The Red-Eared Ghosts

The Red-Eared Ghosts

Vivien Alcock

Houghton Mifflin Company
Boston 1997

Copyright © 1997 by Vivien Alcock

All rights reserved. For information about permission
to reproduce selections from this book, write to Permissions, Houghton Mifflin
Company, 215 Park Avenue South,
New York, New York 10003.

First published in Great Britain 1996 by Methuen Children's Books,
an imprint of Reed Books Ltd., Michelin House, 81 Fulham Road,
London SW3 6RB and Auckland, Melbourne, Singapore, and Toronto.

The text of this book is set in Simoncini Garamond.

Library of Congress Cataloging-in-Publication Data

Alcock, Vivien.
The red-eared ghosts / Vivien Alcock.
p.   cm.
Summary: Mary Frewin has seen "ghosts" since she was a baby
and after learning about her great-great grandmother
and stumbling through a time wreck near
her home in London, she understands why.

RNF ISBN 0-395-81660-2   PAP ISBN 0-395-88394-6
[1. Space and time—Fiction.]
I. Title.   PZ7.A334Rj   1997
[Fic]—dc20   96-1209   CIP   AC

Printed in the United States of America
BP   10   9   8   7   6   5   4   3   2   1

To Jane, Jess, and Julian, with love.

1

There was something odd about Mary Frewin. Something funny, to use one of her favorite words. Not that you could tell just by looking at her. She was quite a pretty girl, if you didn't mind bright orange hair and a few freckles. There was nothing wrong with her eyes now. The nice surgeon at the hospital had put them right for her years ago, when she was small.

Mary Frewin had been born with her eyes wildly askew. When she lay in her pram and looked at her mother with her right eye, her left eye gazed way out over Mrs. Frewin's head toward the corner of the sitting room ceiling where the damp came through.

"That's the cause of it," Mrs. Frewin said gloomily. She was a small woman with quick eyes, like a nervous bird. "Seeing two different places at the same time is bound to upset a baby. A man on

TV the other night said small children don't forget easy. You think they have, but years later they throw up everything that disagreed with them like a cat."

"What are you talking about?" Mr. Frewin asked, without looking up from his newspaper.

"Our daughter. I'm worried about her."

"Nothing wrong with Mary that can't be cured," her father said. "Girl's nonsense, that's all it is."

Mrs. Frewin took no notice. She was gazing up at the damp patches on the ceiling. What odd shapes they were. That one looked like the head of a man with a long pointed nose, a fish's gaping mouth, and a receding chin. A horrid face. And that one resembled some sort of beast, a crouching, humpbacked, panting creature. Enough to give anyone the shivers.

"You should've painted the ceiling when I asked you to," she said. "You should've painted over them."

Her husband went on reading his paper and did not answer.

Mrs. Frewin sighed. "Perhaps I ought to go and see her new teacher about her," she suggested.

"No! Let things alone. Don't stir the pot —"

"If you don't stir the pot, things stick to the bottom and burn," Mrs. Frewin told him, from personal experience.

"Good thing, perhaps. Get rid of them once and

2

for all, like you ought to get rid of your great-grandma's book. Supposing Mary found it —"

"She won't. I've hidden it too well."

"Well, don't show it to her teacher. No need to tell her new teacher anything. What's her name now?"

"Timpson," his wife told him. "Miss Timpson."

Miss Freda Timpson was a brand-new teacher, young and hopeful. She liked to think that everyone was born with a talent for something, even the pupils of class 7F. She refused to be discouraged by their dismal schoolwork. Somewhere in each of those thick heads, she thought kindly, was an individual spark of genius waiting to be discovered — by her.

"We all have the ability to do something really well, if we work hard enough," she told them, to cheer them up. "We must try and find out —"

Her gaze, which had been wandering over the faces in front of her, stopped abruptly. At the back, she saw the circle of a huge yawn beneath a tangle of orange hair: Mary Frewin.

There was something about the girl that irritated Miss Freda Timpson like chicken pox.

"I'm sorry if I'm boring you, Mary. Perhaps you don't agree with me?"

"Yes, Miss."

"You mean you do agree that each of us has a special talent?"

"Yes, Miss."

The girl's voice was flat. No flicker of interest showed on her pale face. To catch her eye was like catching a cold; her gaze seemed to suck out all Miss Timpson's own energy and enthusiasm. She could not resist saying sharply, "Then perhaps you'd be kind enough to let us know what your own particular talent is, Mary, for I haven't been able to discover the slightest sign of one."

"I can see ghosts, Miss," Mary Frewin said.

The class laughed. Miss Freda Timpson controlled her temper with an effort and said mildly, "At least you have a vivid imagination. Perhaps you can apply it to your schoolwork in the future."

"Yes, Miss," the girl said, and the shadow of some emotion at last showed on her face — disappointment.

I've failed her in some way, Miss Timpson thought. She wasn't trying to be funny. There's something troubling her, but what?

She did not like feeling she had failed any child in her care. So when that evening on her way home from school, she saw Mary Frewin sitting on a bench by the canal, she stopped and spoke to her.

4

"Hullo, Mary."

"Hullo, Miss."

"All by yourself tonight? What's happened to your friends?" (Had Mary any friends? Miss Timpson wondered uneasily.)

"I'm waiting for some," the girl said, in her flat voice.

Miss Timpson was touched. She sat down beside her, wondering if she could get the girl to talk.

"Are you happy at school, Mary?" she asked.

"Yes, Miss."

"No problems with your work?"

"No, Miss."

"No trouble at home?"

"No, Miss."

Did the girl ever say anything else but "Yes, Miss, No, Miss"? Miss Timpson wondered. Then she remembered. The girl had claimed to be able to see ghosts. Was that what was worrying her? Perhaps she really believed it. Miss Timpson looked at the pale face beside her. The girl was staring at the cloudy water of the canal, and heaven knew what she thought she was seeing there.

"You're not really frightened of ghosts, are you, Mary?"

"Oh no, Miss. They don't do nothing. They're boring," the girl said with a shrug.

5

"Well, that's certainly an original opinion," Miss Timpson murmured, puzzled. "Perhaps you think it's all nonsense, as I do."

Mary did not answer. She was staring at the water and frowning. Suddenly she turned and looked accusingly at Miss Timpson. Her face had come alive now. There was color in her cheeks and her black eyes sparkled with anger.

"All that you said about everyone having a talent — what's the point of it? What's the point of me seeing ghosts? It never done me no good. Mum don't like it and Dad says I'm to stop talking crazy. And *nobody's* interested!"

She spoke so bitterly, so unhappily, that Miss Timpson said gently, "I am, Mary. I'm interested."

Someone else was interested. He stood in the shadow of the bridge, a thin faded figure of a man, like a pale stain against the blackened brick. His nose was long and narrow, and his lips were slightly open like a dead cod's. At his feet lay a large wolflike dog. Both dog and man watched Mary Frewin and listened to every word she said, but neither Mary nor Miss Timpson noticed them.

2

A cold wind sprang up from nowhere. It blew around Miss Timpson's neck, making her flesh creep, and set Mary's bright hair flickering like flames against the gray September sky.

"Are you really interested?" Mary asked eagerly.

"Yes, I am. Tell me, when did you first start seeing them?"

"I was born with it, wasn't I?" Mary said. "Like you were saying, that's my talent. Saw 'em when I was in my pram. 'Course, I didn't know they were ghosts then. Just thought they were a funny sort of people. Everything looks funny when you're in your pram, don't it? Big faces making silly noises at you, buses going by like houses on wheels, dogs with funny ears and four feet. How was I to know they were anything special. Thought everyone could see them, didn't I?"

"I see," Miss Timpson said, interested in spite of

her common sense telling her it was all nonsense. "When did you find out —"

"That they were ghosts? Not for ages. I used to call 'em the funny people, see, and nobody knew what I was talking about. 'What funny people?' my mum says. 'You know, the funny people,' I says. We'd go on like that for a bit till she'd get cross and shout at me not to be silly. It was my friend Isobel who said perhaps they were ghosts. Never done me no good, it hasn't," Mary said gloomily. "Even my friends don't want to hear about them no more. Say they're boring. They are, too," she added fairly. "Don't do nothing exciting. No heads tucked under their arms, or bones rattling. Nothing like that. Though there's been a faint clinking lately, coming from behind me. Footsteps and a chain clinking—"

"What was it?"

"I dunno, Miss."

"Couldn't you see anything?"

Mary shivered. "I didn't look around, Miss. Didn't want to, somehow."

"I thought you weren't frightened of them," Miss Timpson said, while the evening sun cast its long shadows and the wind blew more coldly.

"I ain't then! I ain't scared!" Mary cried, her grammar slipping wildly, as it often did when she was excited.

They were both silent for a moment, sitting side by side on the bench overlooking the canal, each wondering what the other was thinking.

Mary had been disappointed so often in the past. Disappointed by everyone, her mother, her teachers, her friends, even by her ghosts themselves. Why was she the only person to see them? For she was, though her friend Nonny sometimes pretended he could almost see them too.

"How can you almost see someone?" she'd demand. "I mean, you either do or you don't."

"I just caught a glimpse," he'd claim, his round ebony eyes peering earnestly at a lamppost, as if willing it to turn into a ghost.

"What did it look like?"

"Um, sort of tall and thin and fuzzy."

"Male or female fuzzy?"

"Difficult to tell."

"I bet. You are a liar, Nonny Richards," she'd said, laughing, knowing he was only pretending to see them to comfort her. She couldn't really blame him if he didn't believe her. Seeing's believing, that's what everyone at school told her. Shut up about your silly ghosts, Mary Frewin. Nobody believes you. Nobody's interested.

Until her new teacher had said so kindly, "I am, Mary. I'm interested."

She looked up at Miss Timpson, who had been

watching her thoughtfully. "What do they look like, Mary, your ghosts?" she asked.

"Funny," Mary said, unable to get away from the word.

"Come, Mary, you can do better than that. You don't mean they tell jokes and make you laugh, do you?"

"No, Miss, not that sort of funny."

"You mean they're peculiar? Odd, strange? In what way, Mary? Try and describe them to me."

"Sort of smudgy," Mary said at last. "Like they were breathed onto the air. Like you could wipe 'em away with your hands, only you can't. I tried. Some of 'em look like they've worn away in patches, just leaving bits of 'em floating in space. Two eyes and half a nose, perhaps. Or a pair of hands waving —"

"*Ugh!* How gruesome!"

"You don't have to be frightened, Miss," Mary said kindly. "Like I told you, they don't do nothing. Just walk by, not seeming to notice I'm there. Oh, and I forgot to say. They got bright red ears."

Miss Timpson didn't know what to do. There was obviously something very wrong with the poor child. She ought to see a doctor. Yet it was surprising how convincing she'd been, until she mentioned the red ears. "Sort of smudgy," she'd said.

"Mary, when did you last have your eyes examined?" Miss Timpson asked.

"Last week, and there's nothing wrong with 'em! I can read the bottom line. I don't squint anymore and I'm not colorblind. He did all the tests, and he said my eyes are fine!" Mary said furiously. *"So there!"*

"Yes, yes, all right," Miss Timpson said hastily, looking around in embarrassment. She did not notice the man standing in the shadow of the bridge, holding his ragged black dog on a chain. She only saw two women walking along the footpath, looking back over their shoulders. "Please don't shout, Mary. I didn't mean to upset you. I just wondered if there might be a rational explanation —"

"You think I'm crazy?" Mary asked, sick with disappointment. "You're just like everybody else. *Horrible!*"

"No, Mary, listen! Of course I don't think you're crazy. Only it's easy to be mistaken. I remember once thinking I saw an old bent woman at the foot of our stairs. I was sure of it. I'd have sworn to it in a court of law. Do you know what it turned out to be? My mother's coat and scarf that she'd left hanging over the banister. It's easy to be mistaken."

"Yes, Miss," Mary said flatly, getting to her feet.

Now I've really upset her, Miss Timpson thought unhappily. She'll never forgive me, and I only wanted to help her. "Mary, please, let's talk some more. Perhaps we could go to a café."

"I gotta go, Miss. My friends are waiting for me over there. Look! In the shadows of that tree."

Miss Timpson did not see anyone at first. The sun had gone in, and it was getting dark. Shadows moved over the footpath and wriggled on the stagnant water of the canal. Then she saw in the deepest shadow the smudge of a figure. Everything about it was pale and indistinct, the hair, the face, the dress. And beside it, about level with its shoulders, she saw with horror a pair of disconnected eyes, floating in space.

3

Much to her shame, Miss Timpson screamed; only a small scream, it's true, muffled by her hand as soon as two children stepped out of the shadow and she saw they were not ghosts.

One was a girl of about twelve, tall and thin. She was wearing a shiny white plastic raincoat. Her long hair was flaxen, her brows hardly showed against her pale skin, and her white lashes shadowed the palest green eyes Miss Timpson had ever seen. The other was a boy of about the same age, only much shorter, so that his head came only to the girl's shoulder. His skin was so dark that from where Miss Timpson stood, only his bright black eyes showed up in his shadowed face. These eyes, far from floating in space, stared at her steadily.

"Oh," she said, flushing.

The three children looked at her and giggled.

13

"Are you all right? Is anything the matter?" a voice called out from behind her.

She turned around.

The man with the dog stepped back out of sight. It was a younger man who spoke. He was standing on the bridge, looking down at her, a tall young man with a riot of light brown hair that curled over the top of his head and right round his chin, giving him the appearance of someone peering through an autumn hedge. Small round spectacles balanced insecurely on his nose.

"Why, it's Freda Timpson," he said, recognizing her. "What's the matter?"

"Nothing." Why did he have to come now? she thought. She'd looked out for him for so long, glancing at every face she passed, hoping it would turn out to be his. Why did he have to turn up just in time to see her make a fool of herself?

"But you screamed. I heard you."

She went a deeper shade of pink, conscious that the children were watching them. "Oh, I — I stepped on something sharp. It's nothing, honestly."

"Better let me have a look."

"No, please don't bother —"

But it was too late. He'd left the bridge and was coming, bounding down the steps to the footpath.

14

She looked at the children and said as firmly as she could, "Good night."

"Good night, Miss," Mary Frewin called, and her two friends echoed, " 'Night, Miss," and to her relief they all ran off.

"Are they three of your children?" the young man asked, looking after them. "Nice kids. Now sit down on this bench and let me have a look at your foot. What's the matter? Don't you recognize me?"

"Yes, but —"

"I'm perfectly respectable, I assure you. You did your teacher-training in my school, remember? We sat next to each other in the cafeteria, and I took you to feed the ducks on the canal. Edward Potts. The kids call me Potty, of course, or worse. Don't say you've forgotten me already! I flattered myself we got on rather well together. I'd have asked you out, only my girlfriend wouldn't have liked it. It must be my new beard. I suspected it might be a mistake. Shall I shave it off? I will if you like."

"Yes. No. I don't know," she said, laughing and confused.

"How's your foot? Is it bleeding? Let me see."

"There's nothing wrong with it," Freda confessed.

"Then why did you scream?"

"I thought I saw — oh, Edward, I've made such a fool of myself. I wanted to help one of my girls, but I think I've just made things worse. I'll never live it down."

"Come to the pub, and tell me all about it. You can cry on my shoulder, if you like," he said kindly. "I can't say fairer than that."

"Is your girlfriend going to be there?" she asked, not wanting to meet her.

"*Her?* No. She went back to visit her parents in Scotland, met her childhood sweetheart, and the next thing I know is I get a wedding invitation through the post. Come on, Freda, let's go to the pub and exchange sad stories."

"Can you see her?" Mary Frewin asked.

"They're going off together," Nonny said, his bright black eyes peering through the holly leaves. "He's holding her elbow. Now he's smiling down at her."

"Is she the teacher you dote on?" Isobel asked, pushing her long flaxen hair back from her face. She was always fiddling with her hair, pushing it this way or that, sucking the ends of it, braiding it in her fingers.

16

"I don't dote on her. I hate her!" Mary said angrily.

"Since when? You're always on about her, how she's the best ever. You talk nice like her when you remember to. You copy her handwriting."

"So all right, I liked her. Not anymore," Mary said bitterly. "She's as bad as the others. Worse. I told her all about my ghosts and she pretended to be interested, like she believed me. Then she asked me when I'd last had my eyes tested! I hope she's hurt her foot real bad."

"She's not limping," Isobel told her, looking around the holly bush behind which they were hiding. "I don't believe she hurt it at all."

"Why did she scream then?"

"If you ask me, she likes him. He's not bad looking, is he? I expect she hoped he'd lift her up in his arms and carry her home. She should've gone on a diet first."

"She's not fat."

"She's not exactly thin either. Look, they're holding hands now."

"How stupid," Mary muttered.

"He's only helping her up the steps," Nonny told her.

Nonny knew Mary had liked her new teacher, whatever she said now. He knew also how sensitive she was about her ghosts and the fact that nobody but she could see them. He'd tried his best, staring so hard into space that sometimes the air seemed to shift in front of his eyes as if on the point of revealing something new and strange. But it never happened. He'd blink and the world would be back in its old place again, dull and ordinary. "Do you know why I think Miss Timpson screamed?" he asked.

"No. Why?"

"I think she thought we were ghosts. Just for a minute. Just till she saw us properly. She looked frightened."

"She doesn't believe in ghosts, Nonny," Mary told him drearily. "Not my ghosts anyway."

"She will," Nonny said. "She will by the time we've finished with her."

"What d'you mean?"

"I've got an idea," he said.

It wasn't true. He only said it because she looked so miserable and he wanted to cheer her up. He could think of no way of making her teacher believe in her ghosts. It was all he could do to believe in them himself.

"Tell me, Nonny. Do tell me," she cried, her eyes bright again.

But he couldn't think of anything on the spur of

the moment. "Wait till we get home," he said. "Let's meet after tea. I'll tell you then, I promise."

They went off together, walking quickly for they were already late. The man with the dog stepped out of the shadows under the bridge and watched them go.

4

Mary, Isobel, and Nonny lived in adjoining apartments on the top floor of Cloudsley Towers, a high-rise block three streets away from the canal. When they'd been too small to be allowed out by themselves, they had played in the long passage outside their front doors. Or, they sat at the top of the concrete stairs, listening to the sounds of the building; the creaking of the elevators going up and down, the distant radios, the occasional shuffle of Mrs. Dobbie's tired feet in the passage below, and the shouts of the older children returning home from school.

"Bad boys, bad boys!" they'd hear Mrs. Dobbie yelling, as boys from the ninth floor went whooping past, nearly knocking her over. Once, becoming confused, she'd shouted, "Bad dogs! Bad dogs!" and the boys began frisking around her, barking and pawing at her clothes.

Hearing them, Mary had laughed, but now that the boys were older and meaner, she tried to keep out of their way.

"You're late," Mrs. Frewin complained, when Mary arrived home.

"I waited for Isobel and Nonny. You told me to."

"I wish I could've got you into their school, but I put it off till the last minute and it was full," her mother said. "I don't like you coming back on your own. That rough gang — what do they call themselves?"

"The Bad-Dog Boys."

"They're always hanging around, looking for trouble. Somebody ought to do something about them."

"They don't bother me."

"You sure? Only if they did, I'd make your dad do something," Mrs. Frewin said fiercely. "Report them to somebody. Tell the town council. Write to our mayor. If I wasn't so busy I'd do it myself."

"It's all right. They only call out rude names when they got nothing better to do." They called her Spooky Loonie and threatened to make a ghost of her, but she wasn't going to tell her mother that. "They'd never dare touch us when Nonny's there. He's got clout," she said.

"Nonny Richards? But he's a shrimp of a boy."

"Maybe he is, but he's got two enormous older

brothers and the biggest father on the block. And he's got a cousin who's been chosen to throw the shot in the Olympics."

Her mother looked hurt. "You've got your dad. He may only have one arm, thanks to serving his country, but he's a big man. Six feet in his socks. And he wears a uniform."

"Yeah, I know, Mum."

Her father had been an army sergeant before he was invalided out. He now worked as a doorman outside the Majestic Hotel and had a purple uniform speckled with gold buttons, which he wore as proudly as he'd ever worn the Queen's khaki. He seemed to think he looked good in it. The Bad-Dog Boys called him General Plum and saluted him when they passed the hotel, shrieking with laughter behind his back.

"He may not have been chosen for the Olympics, but your dad played football for his school," her mother said.

Mary laughed. "And you won the egg-and-spoon race. Yeah, I know, Mum. But it ain't quite the same. Hey, what d'you think my new teacher said today?"

"I dunno. What?" Mrs. Frewin asked uneasily. In her experience, teachers wanting to talk to you meant trouble.

"She said everyone was born with a gift, a special talent, and she asked me what mine was —"

"Mary! You didn't go and tell her about your ghosts!"

"Yes, I did. Why shouldn't I?"

"It's just — well, it makes people think that you're odd."

Mary shrugged. "I don't care. Anyway, she didn't believe me. Nobody believes me, except Nonny —" she paused, then added slowly, "and maybe you. I sometimes feel you do, whatever you say." She tried to see through the mask of makeup that gave her mother a doll's face, hiding her true expression. "You ever seen a ghost, Mum? Is that it?"

"No, not me," her mother said truthfully, but her eyes went to the stains on the ceiling, and it seemed to her that the one that looked like a man with a long pointed nose was darker than before.

"Mum, you're hiding something from me, aren't you?" Mary asked.

"No, of course not," Mrs. Frewin said, but she thought of her great-grandmother's book. It would never do for Mary to find it. Her husband was right. She'd have to get rid of it. Seemed a pity to burn it, though. It was old. It might be valuable.

"I can't waste time in idle chatter," she said firmly. "Come on. You're to have your tea with

Isobel today. I must be off. I've got two perms and a color job to do this evening and your dad's working late —"

"Oh, Mum, that's the second time this week. It isn't fair for me to be eating their food all the time. I try not to eat too much, but I get *hungry*."

"You're a growing girl. It's only natural. And Lucy Frayne doesn't mind. She's always pleased to see you. She told me so."

"Is that true?" Mary knew her mother was not above telling little lies. White lies, she called them, though some of them could do with a wash.

"True as I'm standing here," her mother told her, without blushing. "Only today she said, 'I'm always pleased to see your Mary.' Now run along, I must be off. Bye, love." She kissed Mary, leaving a smudge of lipstick on her cheek, wiped it off with a licked finger, and pushed her out of the door.

Mary liked going to Isobel's apartment. Isobel's mother, Lucy Frayne, was a pale, pretty woman. She worked for a theatrical costumer and often brought home garments that needed a few stitches: dresses glittering like goldfish with sequins, or studded all over with glass diamonds and emeralds and rubies, soldiers' scarlet uniforms, judges' wigs that were coming unravelled, and once a cat costume that the moths had got at.

When the girls were small, she used to give them spare sequins, a glass jewel or two, and scraps of silk and velvet and lace for their dolls. Now that they were older, she gave them tea and sandwiches and cream cake and entertained them with gossip about the people at work and their neighbours in Cloudsley Towers.

"I love your mum," Mary told Isobel after their tea, when they went out to sit on the stairs and wait for Nonny. "I wish she was mine."

"She's all right, but nobody's perfect."

"What do you mean?"

"Just don't tell her any secrets."

"You mean she'd tell?"

"It wasn't me who told everybody about your ghosts. And it wasn't Nonny. It was my mum. She can't help it. She doesn't mean to, but she's got a slippery tongue."

"My mum's got a mouth like a prison. She don't let nothing out. I know she's hiding something from me. One day I'm going to search her wardrobe and find it."

"You mean it's an object? Not just something she knows and you don't?"

"It's a thing, all right. And it's in their room. She

keeps telling me to knock before I open the door, and when I forget, she gets cross and flustered and bundles me out before I got a chance to look around. And now she's taken to locking her wardrobe. But one day she's going to forget."

"Let's go and see if she has," Isobel suggested, her face brightening. Like her mother, she was curious. "You've got your own key, haven't you? Here's Nonny. He'll help us search. You can trust us. We won't tell, will we, Nonny?" she said, and explained to him quickly what they'd been talking about.

Mary didn't want them to help her search. There was no telling what they might find. It might be something terrible. Something dark and private that nobody must ever know.

"There isn't time now," she said. "I want to hear all about your idea, Nonny."

Nonny sat down on the step beside her. "You probably won't think much of it," he said sheepishly. "I thought Isobel could dress up in one of her mum's historical costumes and drift about in the mist —"

"What mist?"

"There's usually a mist coming off the canal first thing in the morning."

"I'm not coming out of the canal first thing in the morning, thank you, Nonny," Isobel told him. "Nor any other time. The water's filthy. It's probably poisonous. Besides, her teacher saw me this afternoon. She'd recognize me —"

"Not if you made up your face," Nonny said. "Loads of mascara around your eyes and lipstick and rouge and Mrs. Frewin's black wig, and I bet you wouldn't know yourself in the mirror. You're so tall, you'd look grown-up."

Isobel began to look interested. She liked dressing up. "I'd have to stuff something down my bra."

"Do you wear a bra?" Mary asked, surprised, for her friend was as thin and flat as a blade of grass.

"Why shouldn't I? Lots of girls in my class do. Why shouldn't I wear a bra if I want to?"

"No reason at all," Mary said hastily, seeing that Isobel was offended.

"What do you think of my plan?" Nonny asked.

"It stinks," Isobel said flatly.

"It isn't so bad," Mary said kindly. "But — you see, it wouldn't really help. It would just be a trick. I wanted somebody to believe me. I wanted somebody, *anybody*, to see one of my ghosts. Just so I'll know I'm not mad."

They were silent for a moment. Someone was playing a radio on the floor below. The music drifted up the concrete stairs; a thin plaintive voice was singing.

27

"And I will never, never, never,
Never see him more . . ."

Nonny said at last, "I got an idea. Why don't you try and make friends with one of your ghosts, Mary, and get it to help you. Talk to it nicely. See if you can persuade it to make itself visible to your teacher."

Mary did not like Nonny's new idea any better than his first. He did not know what her ghosts were like. Slippery, that's what they were. Try and catch one, and it slid by you like a stray cat. Walk right up to one, and it wasn't there any more but behind you. Shout into its scarlet ear, and it didn't hear you. Or pretended not to.

Then she remembered the footsteps she often heard behind her when she was alone. Footsteps and the clink of a chain. Perhaps next time, she'd turn around and challenge whomever was there . . . if she dared.

5

Mary left the others early, saying she had home-work to do. Actually, she meant to try and pick the lock of her mother's wardrobe door with some bent wire. She went into the room and looked around.

She was glad she hadn't let her friends come with her. Isobel would have laughed at the moth-eaten teddy bear wearing pink baby clothes that sat on the pillows of her parents' double bed. She would have nudged Nonny when she thought Mary wasn't looking and pointed to the framed photograph on top of the chest of drawers, which showed Mr. Frewin in his plum-colored uniform, standing proudly to attention in front of the hotel where he worked. On the canopy above his head was written in large red letters THE MAJESTIC HO, the rest of the name being cut off by the edge of the photograph.

The Majestic Ho! Poor Dad. No wonder the Bad-Dog Boys laughed at him. He was far too fat for his tight uniform. The two rows of bright buttons climbed over his stomach like headlights going over a hill.

Why did Mum leave her nightie on the floor for people to trip over? Mary disentangled the nightdress from her feet. Her fingers brushed against something cold and hard on the carpet. She picked it up and stared at it. It was a key.

She stared at it curiously. It was too small to be the key of a door. The key to a trinket box? But her mother kept her jewelery, such as it was, in a plastic cutlery tray in one of her drawers. A suitcase? Wrong sort of key. The wardrobe? No. The key to the wardrobe was in the lock — *the key!*

Trembling with excitement, she turned it and opened the door. Clothes in the middle, shoes on the bottom, and at the top a wide shelf crowded with tumbled bags and boxes, as if somebody in a hurry had been there before her. Spare blankets. An electric fan. The wigs Mum used for work when her hair was a mess. Bags of red wool. What was that shining out like a watching eye from the shadows of Mum's straw hat? Mary brought over the chair and climbed up. She moved aside the hat and there it was, a small shiny keyhole in a black metal box.

She lifted the box down and put it on the bed. It was very heavy, an iron box, unlocked and empty. Whatever her mother had hidden inside was gone. So that was why her mother had left the wardrobe open today and carelessly dropped the small key to the box on the floor. There was nothing for Mary to find anymore. Her mother had taken it away.

Mary sat on the bed, staring at the black box. She had seen it before, long ago. Memories drifted into her mind . . .

She had been sitting here, swinging her legs, which had then been too short to reach the floor. The sun had been shining.

"What's in that black box on the chest of drawers, Mum?"

"Nothing."

"Why's it locked then?"

"To stop nosy little girls like you from poking and prying into other people's concerns."

"Where's the key?"

"Never you mind. And don't you go trying to open it, Miss. There's nasty things in there that'd bite your fingers."

"What sort of things?"

"Snakes and spiders and long-legged —"

"Don't go frightening the child, Bridie," her dad had said, putting his arm around Mary. "There's nothing in there, love. Only a dull old book and papers and things."

It must have been after this that her mother had hidden the box.

How could I have forgotten it? she wondered. Did Dad make it sound boring on purpose? An old book, old papers. What papers? Perhaps they're about me, she thought. Perhaps they explain why I was born different.

The two teachers had left the pub and were now sitting in the Happy Dragon Café beneath the pink Chinese lanterns, eating their supper and talking. They were not talking about Mary Frewin; they were talking about themselves. Their eyes were shining and they looked happy.

Edward Potts was eating with chopsticks. Every now and then he scattered fried rice all over the pink tablecloth.

"Sorry. Some's gone in your glass. Here, let me fish it out for you. There you are. All gone now," he said, licking a grain of rice off his little finger. "Now, tell me about this girl you're worried about. What's her name again?"

"Mary Frewin."

"The ghost girl. You say she claims to have seen them ever since she was a baby? How often? Every day? Once a week? Or what?"

"I don't know. I didn't want to ask her," Freda Timpson told him. "It was a little difficult."

"Difficult?" He looked puzzled. He obviously wasn't a young man who ever found it difficult to ask anything he wanted to know. "Do you mean it upset her to talk about them?"

"Not exactly. I just didn't know whether it was a good idea to ask her too many questions."

"Why ever not? How else can one find things out?" Edward waved his chopsticks in the air. "Sorry. Some rice has gone on your blouse. Just there — I hope it hasn't left a mark?"

"It'll wash out."

"I'm sorry. I'm not doing very well, am I? I'd better use this," he said, putting down his chopsticks and picking up a fork from the table. "You were saying you found it difficult to ask her questions. Why?"

"I thought girls of her age can be very sensitive — emotional — you know how it is. I didn't know whether I ought to encourage her to talk about it. Some people mightn't think it was a very healthy subject —"

"Whatever can you mean? What isn't a healthy subject?" he asked, staring at her in astonishment.

33

"Well, ghosts and things like that," she said, flushing.

"Really, Freda, that's utter nonsense. How can there be anything unhealthy about the supernatural?"

"Easily," she retorted sharply. "If ghosts were healthy, they wouldn't all be dead!"

He laughed uproariously, as if she'd made a joke, and after a moment, she couldn't help laughing, too.

"I've always been fascinated by the paranormal," he told her. "I read quite a lot about it when I was at college. I can't understand how some people can dismiss it without even having made a study of the subject. They must be completely earthbound. No imagination. I wish I could meet your Mary Frewin. Seriously, I think it would be good for her to talk about it. From what she told you, I gather her parents are not very sympathetic, nor her friends. If she's genuine — and I gather you think she is, don't you, Freda?"

She hesitated, somehow not wanting to tell him that she didn't believe in ghosts. He might be disappointed in her. He'd lump her in with all the other people who were earthbound. Earthbound. It sounded so unattractive, like someone plodding heavily through the mud in clunky green boots and never looking up at the sky.

"I think she's telling the truth, as she sees it —" she began slowly.

"None of us can do more than that!" he interrupted. "Poor kid, she must feel terribly alone. Don't you think it would do her good to talk to two kind and friendly teachers like us?"

She looked at him and smiled. It was true. He was kind and friendly, and very sweet. The light from the pink Chinese lanterns shone on his brown hair and reflected like rose petals in his spectacles. She remembered how he'd helped her when she was a shy student, doing her teacher-training in the school where he taught.

Mary needs someone to believe in her ghosts and I can't, she thought. Perhaps Edward can help her.

"You don't think I ought to talk to her parents first?" she asked.

"No! She'd see it as a betrayal. Sneaking. You know what kids are like. You'd never get her to trust you again. Never!" He thumped his fist on the table. A small piece of chicken teriyaki flew off his fork, sailed over Freda's left shoulder, and landed on the empty table behind her. They both began to laugh.

"I'm hopeless, aren't I? I've always been clumsy. My mother says she dreads taking me out anywhere respectable. Things simply fly out of my hands. I'm sorry, Freda. I've no right to interfere. Why don't you tell me to mind my own business?"

"I need all the help I can get. I started badly with Mary," she confessed. "She used to irritate me, the way she kept staring at me and yawning, as if she found me a bore. But one of the teachers told me that some parents let their kids stay up till all hours of the night, so she's probably just tired. Tippy says she's often had kids dropping off to sleep the moment she turns her back. Mind you, I've heard she's not a very good teacher. But I want to be, Edward. They're all such nice kids in my class. I don't want to let them down."

He smiled at her enthusiasm. "Good. Let's drink a toast." Picking up his wine glass, he held it up toward her. "To us. To the protectors of Mary Frewin," he said. "Together we'll save her from her ghosts."

The light from the Chinese lanterns shone down on their lifted glasses, giving the white wine curved pink shadows, like listening ears.

6

The next day was bright but colder. The September wind blew yellow leaves off their twigs and tugged at Mrs. Frewin's russet curls as if mistaking her for a walking bush.

"Drat this wind. It'll have my wig off and blow it halfway down the street," she muttered. Better take it off and put it in my pocket. It wouldn't do to lose it. That was the worst of working in a hairdresser's. You always had to look just so, and she never seemed to have time to do her own hair properly.

It was her lunch hour and she was taking her great-grandmother's book to Pepper's, the local secondhand bookshop. She should have got rid of it before, family heirloom or not, but somehow she couldn't just put it in the dustbin. It wouldn't seem right. This was a better way.

The bookshop was dark after the bright street.

Mr. Pepper appeared out of the shadows, a thin middle-aged man who, in her professional opinion, needed a haircut badly.

"Please feel free to browse," he said with a smile.

"I'm not buying. I've got something here I'd like to sell. A book. An old book. A very old book. Antique," she added hopefully.

"Is it a first edition?" he asked, interested.

"No, it's a book," she said, thinking he hadn't heard her properly. She rummaged in her bag and brought out a thin volume in a mottled green cover.

He took it from her, opened it, read a little here and there, then shut it again, saying apologetically, "I'm afraid there isn't much call for this sort of thing. I couldn't offer you more than fifty pence."

"*Fifty pence!* But my great-grandma's in it. Mary Coram, that's her. It's all about her and every word true, though you might not believe it, and I'm sure I wouldn't blame you, because it's a strange story."

"I'm sorry, but —"

"What about a pound? Though she'd turn in her grave if she knew I was letting her go so cheap."

"Why don't you keep it for your children?" he suggested.

"No! You don't understand — I got to get rid of

it. Here, you have it. Give me whatever you like, but just take it! And don't put it in the window. Hide it in a dark corner somewhere. I don't want her seeing it."

Mr. Pepper stared at her in astonishment, wondering if she was mad.

"All right. Fifty pence then," she said, thrusting it into his hands.

He gave her a pound, not because he thought the book was worth it, but because he was sorry for her, poor crazy women with her doll's face and her scrappy bleached hair standing on end.

"You've got a bargain there," she told him, feeling lightheaded with relief now that he'd taken the book. She'd always hated it. She couldn't think why she hadn't got rid of it sooner.

"There's my bus coming," she cried happily, catching sight of it through the window. She ran toward the door just as a bearded young man came charging in. They crashed together. With a squeal of impatience, she disentangled herself from him, muttering, "My bus, my bus."

"Sorry. Terribly clumsy of me. I hope —" he began, but she didn't wait to hear what he hoped. She was off, running after the bus.

Edward Potts blinked and straightened his spectacles, which had been knocked sideways. Something caught his eye. He looked down.

"Argh!" he cried in horror.

A small furry animal was clinging to the bottom of his jacket. It was like no animal he'd ever seen before. It hung limply as if dead, its small body covered with horrible glistening fur.

"I think it's caught on your button," the book-seller said. "Here, let me remove it for you."

He bent down and carefully detached the creature, leaving a few red-brown hairs behind. Then he held it up, and Edward saw that it wasn't an animal at all, but a wig, covered with fat nylon curls.

"Is it yours, sir?" Mr. Pepper asked.

"Good grief, no! Do I look as if I need a wig? It must've been that woman's."

"She wasn't wearing it when she came in." The bookseller told him. "I particularly noticed because her hair was standing on end. It was bleached. Going dark at the roots. Not that color at all."

"Well, I certainly wasn't wearing it when I came in, I can assure you. I've got enough hair of my own."

"What shall I do with it?" Mr. Pepper asked.

"Don't you know who the woman is?"

"Never seen her before. Oh well, perhaps she'll come back, though she didn't seem exactly at home with books."

"Why don't you put it in the window, so it'll catch her eye if she passes?" Edward suggested.

"Good idea. I'll do that. Now, how can I help you, sir?"

Edward told him that he was looking for something on the paranormal.

"Over there, sir. Between Omens and Psychology," Mr. Pepper told him. "Or you might be interested in this little book. Quite a coincidence. I only just bought it from that lady before you came in."

"The lady with the wig?"

"The lady *without* the wig, sir."

Edward took the slim volume with the mottled green cover and glanced at the title: *True Encounters with the Supernatural.*

"The lady said her great-grandmother was in it. Mary Coram, that was the name," the bookseller told him. "Every word of it was true, or so she claimed. I can't vouch for it personally, of course."

"How much did she sell her grandmother for?" Edward asked, laughing.

"I can let you have it for two pounds," Mr. Pepper said.

Edward opened the book. There was a daguerreotype of Mary Coram opposite the title page. She was wearing a severe dark dress that looked like some sort of uniform, and her curly hair was put up in a heavy knot on the top of her head, as if to keep her down. Her mouth drooped and her big black eyes stared out at Edward sadly, without hope. She looked like a frightened child.

Not finding anything else, he bought it. The face reminded him of somebody, somebody he had seen recently, but he could not think who it was.

7

Isobel was waiting for Mary on the bridge overlooking the canal.

"You're late," she accused. She looked cold. Her pale hair was blowing over her face, and her shoulders were hunched.

"Sorry."

"If we're not careful, we'll run straight into the Bad-Dog Boys," Isobel said. "There's no point in hurrying now. We'd better give them time to go in for their tea. Let's get out of this wind. I'm frozen."

She did, in fact, look rather like an icicle, long and thin and bluish, in her tight faded jeans.

"Do you want to borrow my sweater?" Mary asked.

"No. Frankly I wouldn't be seen dead in it."

She was cross. Mary felt her own temper rising. All right. Be like that. See if I care.

But she did care. She didn't want to quarrel with

Isobel now. She had something to tell her. "It wasn't my fault," she said, after they'd walked halfway down the street in silence. "Miss Timpson kept me. She wants me to come and meet a friend of hers tomorrow after school, who might be able to help me. He's an expert."

"An expert on what?" Isobel asked.

"Ghosts," Mary said.

Isobel sniffed loudly. Perhaps she had a cold.

"She'd told him all about mine," Mary went on, "What cheek! 'I hope you don't mind, Mary,' she said. Of course I minded. I'm fussy whom I tell about my ghosts. I wish I'd never told *her*. We're to have tea with him in the Singing Kettle, if Mum agrees. But I'm not telling Mum."

"Who is this expert of hers?"

"A Mr. Edward Potts —"

"Him!" Isobel screeched. "Potty's no expert. He teaches us math. I told you he teaches at our school, didn't I?"

"No."

"Well, he does. You'd better warn Miss Timpson about him. Everyone knows he changes his girlfriends like library books, and they all end up in tears. He takes them to that Chinese restaurant with the pink lanterns. I saw him there with our art teacher last term. They were sitting in the window and she was crying into a pink paper napkin."

"Perhaps the food's bad there," Mary suggested.

"Idiot! He breaks their hearts," Isobel told her. She and her mother were great readers of romantic fiction. "So your teacher had better watch it. I bet he's just pretending to be an expert to get on her good side. Expert in ghosts, indeed! Nobody in their right mind believes in ghosts."

She hadn't meant to insult Mary. She said it without thinking. But it was enough to start a quarrel on a cold, windy day, with both of them feeling on edge.

It ended up with Isobel walking off in a huff, saying she was going to call on her aunt and not asking Mary to go with her. It was not until she had rounded the corner that she remembered it would mean Mary would have to face the Bad-Dog Boys on her own. She hesitated, wondering whether to run back. She turned, and the wind blew grit into her face. She blinked rapidly, her eyes watering. For a minute she thought she saw a man with a large ugly dog on the corner. Then they were out of sight. Isobel didn't like big dogs. She often crossed the road to avoid them.

"Mary will be all right," she muttered to herself and walked on.

* * *

Mary stood gazing into the window of the second-hand bookshop, pretending she wasn't waiting for Isobel to return. They'd quarreled before on their way home and Isobel had always come back for her, saying irritably, "Oh, come on. We'd better stick together."

But Isobel didn't come back. Mary waited, getting colder. Isobel wouldn't come back now. She'd been too long. I don't care. I'm not afraid of the Bad-Dog Boys. They won't do nothing to me. It's her they're after, with her long blonde hair. I hope they tie it in knots. I hope they steal her pocket money and eat her lemon candy that she keeps in her pockets and never offers — *What's that!*

She'd been staring into the window blindly. Must've been looking straight at it without seeing what it was. Her heart began drumming. Among the books in the shadowy window, she thought she saw a decapitated head, stuck on a stand, the flesh of its face blotched with green like rotting cheese. Then she realized that it was only a globe of the world, onto which somebody had put her mother's second-best wig. Leaning against the stand was a printed notice saying: HAS ANYONE LOST THIS WIG? PLEASE INQUIRE INSIDE.

From behind her came the soft clink of a chain.

She turned around and saw a man standing on the pavement close to her. A tall man, with a long pointed nose, the tip bent to one side as if it had been tweaked by iron fingers. He was smiling, a small, ingratiating smile. On a chain by his side he held a large black hunched dog. Its mouth was also open, showing its yellow teeth.

"It geev me a bad shock." The man spoke with a foreign accent. "I quite thought eet was a cuff-off head, didn't you?"

"Go away!" Mary said.

"Forgeev me. I didn't mean to startle you —"

"Get lost!" she cried, her voice rising shrilly. She bolted into the shop, slamming the door behind her.

"Careful," Mr. Pepper said, rising from the chair on which he'd been sitting. "You'll break the glass, slamming it like that. Why, what's the matter? You're not going to pass out on me, are you? Here, sit down and put your head between your knees."

"That man!" Mary whispered. "Is he still there?"

"What man? Where?" He opened the shop door and looked out into the street. "I can't see anyone. Only two women buying oranges from the grocer next door. You don't mean him, do you? Eddie. Short and fat and wearing a green smock?"

"No. A man with a dog."

"Then he must've made off around the corner.

47

Why? Was he bothering you? Look, if you give me your telephone number, I could ring and ask your mother to come and fetch you. Would that be a good idea?" Mr. Pepper asked.

"She won't be home yet."

"Oh dear," Mr. Pepper said helplessly. "What shall I do with you? You don't look at all well."

"I'll be all right in a minute."

"Something frightened you, didn't it? Was it something the man did? Or said?"

"I dunno —"

She hadn't known whether the man with the dog was a real person or a ghost. She'd always been able to tell before. It was like treading on a step that wasn't there anymore: it had jolted her bones, shaken her brain, unhinged her knees so that she was glad to sit on Mr. Pepper's chair.

Unlike her ghosts, the man had looked solid; the dog, too, with his yellow eyes and rough black hair, had had a true doggy smell. But the man's ears had been scarlet — thin, transparent ghost ears, with the light shining through them.

"If he's been bothering you, perhaps you ought to tell the police," Mr. Pepper said.

She didn't want to talk to the police. What could she say? "It was the wig in the window! The one on the globe. The man said it looked like a cut-off head, and I thought it was, too."

"Good heavens! Yes, I see. It does look rather gruesome. I'm sorry. It was stupid of me," Mr. Pepper apologized, leaning forward and lifting the wig off the globe. "Enough to give anyone a fright. Such a horrid-looking wig, too —"

"It's my mum's. She got it cheap because they couldn't sell it. It's too big for her really. She's always losing it. Shall I take it?" She held out her hand.

Mr. Pepper looked doubtful, as if it occurred to him that she might be a wig thief. "Are you sure it's your mother's?"

"You can soon tell. The lining in Mum's got torn, and she mended it with yellow thread. And there's an ink stain on one of the back curls."

He checked. "One ink stain. One darn in yellow thread. Yes, right. Here you are."

He gave the wig to Mary, who promptly put it on, extinguishing her own bright hair with fat nylon curls.

"I prefer your own hair. Much nicer," Mr. Pepper told her. "That wig's a most unnatural color. And it's too big for you. Be careful you don't lose it in the wind."

Mary thanked him and left the shop. She was around the corner and halfway down the next street before the wig blew off and she had to go chasing after it. An old woman standing outside

49

the post office stopped it by putting her foot on it. Then she picked it up, shook it to get rid of the dust and dead leaves, and held it out to Mary, saying, "You don't need a wig, dear, with pretty hair like yours."

Two compliments in one afternoon. One from the man in the bookshop — *Bookshop!* What had her mother been doing in a secondhand bookshop? Nothing there but dusty old books — *A boring old book, and some papers* — that's what her dad had said the iron box had contained, the box her mother had hidden, the box her mother had left empty only yesterday, sneaking the book out of the house —

She's sold it to him!

Mary raced back to the bookshop, but she was too late. CLOSED the notice on the door said firmly. She rattled the doorhandle and tapped angrily on the glass in case Mr. Pepper was hiding inside among the shadows.

The grocer next door rose up unexpectedly from his piles of oranges and apples, as if he'd been sleeping on the floor behind them and her knocking had woken him up.

"It's no good doing that. He'll be gone. Always off early on the first Friday of the month. Never misses. Visiting his girlfriend, I expect," he said, winking at Mary. "Won't be back till Monday. Can't it wait till then?"

"Yeah. I suppose so."

I'll go in on Monday morning, she thought. I'll call in before school. I don't care if it makes me late. I'd tell him Mum had no right to sell it. I'll make him give it back to me. If he won't, I'll offer to buy it. Can't be worth much; it's not as if it's new. He can't have already sold it. He hardly ever has customers in there, and the few that come in only stand reading the books behind the shelves. They don't *buy* them. Supposing it's just a boring old book like Dad said. But it can't be. It must be something about me. *Why else would Mum hide it?*

She was thinking so hard about the book that she forgot all about the Bad-Dog Boys. She did not notice them hanging about by the garages, trying to keep out of the wind, bored and restless and looking for trouble. And there she was with her bright orange hair blowing, carrying her school bag in one hand and mother's second-best wig in the other, somebody to tease, somebody to scare a little.

"What you got there, a dead rabbit? Hey, Spooky Loonie, we're talking to you."

She didn't answer. She began to walk more

51

quickly. That was a mistake. It aroused their hunting instincts.

"Spooky Loonie! Spooky Loo-oo-oonie!" they called, and she heard them coming after her. Without glancing around, she raced down the passage toward the elevators, her boots clattering on the stone floor. Please make the elevator be there and waiting. Please let me get there in time to shut them out. Better still, please let some grown-up come, someone big, Nonny's father — or Dad. Dad won't let them hurt me!

But nobody came. When she turned the corner, she saw the elevator door was closing. "Wait for me!" she shouted, running forward. A pair of thin hands appeared in the narrowing gap and forced the gates open.

"Come een, Mary Frewin," the man with the long nose said, his eyes shining like glass.

"No!" Mary shouted and backed away, forcing herself out through the closing doors, straight into the hands of Rottweiler, who grabbed hold of her with a cry of triumph. As the pack closed in, she saw the doors slam shut and heard the elevator begin its slow ascent.

8

Now that the Bad-Dog Boys had got her, they didn't seem to know what to do with her. Rottweiler pushed her toward Pitbull, who pushed her back. The other boys crowded around and stared. Then one of them snatched her mother's second-best wig out of her hand, and they began throwing it to one another, shrieking with laughter. She made no attempt to get it back, which annoyed them. They started jostling her, chanting, "Spooky Loonie! Spooky Loonie!" — all except Rottweiler and Pitbull, who had taken her school bag and were busy pulling the books out and throwing them on the floor.

"Where's yer purse?" Pitbull demanded.

"At home."

"Look at me when I'm speaking to yer," he said angrily. "What's the matter with yer?" By this, he really meant: Why aren't you crying? Why aren't you frightened of me? It maddened him the cool way she let herself be pushed around, all the time looking up over their heads.

She was watching the numbers lighting up as the elevator passed the floors — one . . . two . . . three . . .

"Shut up yer yelling," Pitbull told the members of his gang who were still chanting. When they were quiet, he pushed his face close to Mary's and demanded, "D'yer know 'oo I am?"

Everyone in the apartment building knew him, the leader of the Bad-Dog Boys, a great hulking fifteen year old, with tiny blue eyes in a spotty face. He was a mean boy, though not yet quite as wicked as he thought he was.

"Are yer going to answer me or not?" he shouted.

"Pardon? What was that you said?"

"I asked yer if yer knew 'oo I was?"

His face blocked out her view of the lighted numbers. She had once been frightened of him, but now a greater fear had driven out the lesser. She moved sideways so that she could see the numbers again and said carelessly, "You're the leader of the Bow-Wow Boys." This was what her dad called them, and the name slipped out without her noticing.

Five ... four ... *The lift was coming down again!*

Pitbull, maddened by the contemptuous nickname, would have hit her, but Rottweiler grabbed his wrist and stopped him, saying, "Look at her face. She's frightened."

"Of me?" Pitbull asked hopefully.

"No. Of something she saw. She could've got away from us — she'd nearly made it into the elevator, when suddenly she backs out. As if she's seen something real scary —"

"Wot, worse than us?"

"Yeah, right out of our class. She's been watching the numbers ever since. Look, the elevator's coming down again."

They all stood quietly, watching.

"Three ... two ...

"What is it? What's in there?" Rottweiler asked, taking Mary by the shoulders and shaking her a little.

"Didn't you see him?" she whispered. "The man — the man with the dog? He knew my name. *He's coming for me.*"

He didn't need to shake her now. She was shaking all by herself, her face as white was chalk.

"She's out of her mind. Raving mad," Pitbull said uneasily, moving away from her in case her fear was infectious. "She's not worth bothering about. Let's be off!"

Mary was still staring at the numbers — two . . . one. . . .

As the lift moved toward the ground floor, she whimpered, and the Bad-Dog Boys fled, thundering down the passage in a panic they were never to understand. Only Mary stood as if frozen, until Boxer, a thirteen-year-old boy, with a round, rosy face, shouted, "Come on, Mary! You'll be safer with us. We won't do you no harm —" thus carelessly destroying the bad reputation his gang leaders had cultivated.

She ran after them. Some of them, glancing back and seeing her, increased their speed, so that it looked as if she were chasing them, like a small red fox after a pack of hounds.

Mrs. Frewin came home like a whirlwind, bursting through the front door, rushing from room to room, shouting, "Mary! Mary! *Mary!*"

Mary came out of the kitchen, holding a half-eaten cheese sandwich.

"Mum, you're different! You've gone and dyed your hair. It looks nice."

"Don't try to fool me," Mrs. Frewin cried, fury

and relief drying the tears in her eyes. "What's happened? What've you done?"

"Me? Nothing."

"Nothing! I get home from work and what do I find, scattered all over the passage downstairs, eh? Your schoolbooks! Don't try and deny it. They've got your name on them. Mary Frewin, that's you, isn't it? Look at them!" She thrust the school bag she was carrying into Mary's arms. "Torn, crumpled, covered with dirt — what was I supposed to think?"

"That I'd dropped them," Mary suggested.

"And left them there to be trampled on by a herd of elephants? I thought you'd been murdered, at the very least."

"Oh *Mum*," Mary said, hugging her. "You are an old idiot. It's only my books, not me. You've been crying, haven't you?"

"And if I had, who would blame me? A daughter who treats her schoolbooks like rubbish. A daughter who calls her mother an old idiot, *old* and me only in my thirties —"

"A daughter who's going to make you a cuppa tea."

Mrs. Frewin followed Mary into the kitchen and sat down on the stool with a sigh, kicking off her shoes. "I want an explanation, my girl. What happened? Was it them Bad-Dog Boys? Because if it was —"

"It wasn't!"

Mary had already decided not to give the Bad-Dog Boys away. No point in giving them a grudge against her. They hadn't hurt her. In fact, the one they called Boxer had taken her to the elevators on the far side and seen her home safely, asking questions all the way: "What did you see? What scared you? Was it really a ghost? You looked like one yourself. I never saw nobody so white as you, Mary Frewin. Can you really see ghosts, or are you making it all up?" He had been friendly, however. "See you again," he'd said when he left.

"If it wasn't them boys, who was it? Don't go into a dream, Mary. I'm talking to you. Something made you drop your schoolbooks and leave 'em lying. I want to know what it was."

You wouldn't like it if you knew, Mary thought. You'd get into one of your panics, I know you would. You'd go on and on about it. You'd keep Dad awake all night talking about me, and in the morning you'd both be baggy-eyed and miserable and it would be all my fault.

"It was nothing, only a stray dog near the elevators. I do like your hair, Mum. It looks pretty, dark like that. Better than yellow or red. Softer."

"It's the color I was born with," her mother told

her, happily distracted by the compliment, "or as near as I could get it. Do you really think it suits me?"

Mary told her it looked lovely, and that she wished her hair were dark too. "Where do I get my red hair from, Mum?" she asked.

Her mother was silent for a moment. Then she said, "Your great-great-grandmother had red hair. Or so they said. I never knew her. She'd gone before I was born. You take after her." Her hand began shaking and she put her cup down. "You got to be careful, Mary."

"Me? Why? What d'you mean?"

"I don't want to lose you."

"Mum! You're trembling! What's the matter? You're not going to lose me."

"No. No, of course not. I don't know what I was thinking of. Don't take any notice of me. I'm just being silly." Her mother refused to say any more about it than that. But Mary had noticed that her fingers were still shaking.

9

At four o'clock the next day, Mary and Miss Timpson were walking side by side toward the café where they were to meet Mr. Potts.

Mary had had a bad day. Mr. Pepper, arriving late at the bookshop, hadn't wanted to listen to her. "What book? Who wrote it? Who published it?" he'd demanded irritably. "The book your mother sold me yesterday? My dear child, as far as I know, I've never met your mother."

"You had her wig in your window, the purple one, remember?"

"Oh, that lady. I remember."

He told her he'd already sold the book. No, he didn't know the customer's name. No, he couldn't remember what he looked like, except that he had a beard. No, he couldn't remember what the book was about. Why didn't she ask her mother?

"Run along now or you'll be late for school."

She had raced all the way, along the pavements, through the school gates, down the corridor, and straight into the principal as he stepped out of his study. Whoops! Bad mark, Mary Frewin. More bad marks when her teachers saw her school books, creased and torn and covered with dirt. "How did they get into this state, Mary? What do you mean, you don't know? You must know. It didn't happen when you were asleep, did it?"

Only Miss Timpson was sympathetic. "Poor Mary," she'd said vaguely. "Did you drop them into a puddle? Bad luck." But then she was too happy to be cross. Miss Timpson's eyes were shining. Miss Timpson looked prettier than ever. Miss Timpson, Mary diagnosed gloomily, was in love.

Look at her now, walking down the street as if she were going to heaven instead of to the Café Express, where flies walked over the cakes in the window like animated currants. Look at her smiling at everyone they passed, as if she were in love with the whole world, instead of one Mr. Edward Potts, who was fickle and made all his girl-friends cry. "You ought to warn her," Isobel had said. How?

"What's the matter, Mary? You're not worried about meeting Mr. Potts, are you?"

"No, Miss," Mary replied, then, seeing her chance, added quickly, "It's not *me* who should be worried."

"What do you mean?"

"Nothing."

"You must have meant something," Miss Timpson said reasonably. "Who do you think should be worried? Not Mr. Potts, surely?"

"No, Miss."

"Who, then? You can't mean me?" She laughed as if the idea were absurd.

Mary didn't answer.

"I believe you do mean me," Miss Timpson said slowly, standing still and peering down at her. "Why? Why, Mary?"

"They say he has one girlfriend after another, Miss, and makes them all cry."

"Mary!" Miss Timpson went pink. "I'm not one of his girlfriends."

"No, Miss."

"You shouldn't listen to gossip. It may not even be true."

"No, Miss."

"Don't keep saying 'No, Miss, No, Miss' like a clockwork parrot. Explain yourself. Who told you? Not that it matters. I'm not in the least interested. Mr. Potts can have as many girlfriends as he pleases. It's no concern of ours. Why, there is

Mr. Potts. Don't say any more about this, Mary. You shouldn't repeat gossip."

"No, Miss."

"I don't suppose it's true for a minute," Miss Timpson said, but the light had gone out of her eyes. She looked tired and pale and at least five years older than she'd been a minute ago.

It was a bad beginning. Edward Potts did his best. He ordered them tea and cream cakes and gave them his warmest, most friendly smile. It didn't do him any good.

Miss Timpson, remembering her Shakespeare, thought sadly a man may smile and smile and be a villain. Mary, seeing the white teeth gleaming through his beard, thought of crocodiles in a brown river and scowled at him.

"Haven't I seen you somewhere before?" he asked.

"She was with me by the canal yesterday," Miss Timpson told him, when Mary did not answer.

"Oh yes, of course. You were one of the three children who ran off. I didn't get a proper look at you. Somehow I thought you had dark hair. I must be confusing you with someone else."

The waitress brought a pot of tea, a Coke for Mary, and a plate of cream cakes, which Edward

Potts handed around. Miss Timpson shook her head, Mary chose a jam doughnut, and he took a cream bun, which he held in his fingers, ignoring the fork provided. Miss Timpson, who was wearing her new silk shirt, edged away from him.

Mr. Potts began talking about ordinary things, such as Mary's school and whether she was happy there; was her doughnut good; was she fond of history? Mary put on her most stupid face, eyes blank, mouth ajar. She answered each question with a shrug and a muttered, "S'all right."

"I'm boring you," he said with a rueful smile. "I expect you're wondering why I don't get to the point. Very well, let's talk about ghosts. Can you describe your ghosts to me. What are they like?"

People were always asking her that. It was a silly question, she thought. You might as well ask what people looked like. Her ghosts, in fact, were even more varied. Most people have a head, for instance. Not all her ghosts were so lucky. Some were smudgy and incomplete — a pair of hands, a single eye, a bare foot cut off at the ankle, walking by itself in mid-air.

"They're funny." she told him.

"Mary!" Miss Timpson said reproachfully. "You can do better than that."

"Peculiar, then." Mary replied.

"In what way?"

"They got bits missing. And they don't walk right on the ground," Mary said, picking details at random. "They never look at you, or talk, least most of them don't. And when you walk straight up to them, everything sort of shivers and then they're behind you."

"Fascinating," Mr. Potts remarked, and wrote something down in a small notebook. Mary tried to read the words upside-down but the teapot was in the way. She thought he looked amused, as if he didn't believe her.

"What do they wear?" he asked next.

"Clothes," she muttered sulkily.

"Mary!" Miss Timpson said reprovingly, but Edward Potts was used to sulky children and merely smiled.

"What kind of clothes? Do they look old-fashioned? Long dresses? Frock coats? Tall hats?" he asked, sketching the various garments in the air with his half-eaten bun, out of which cream was oozing dangerously. Miss Timpson shrank further away.

"I've never seen nobody historical," Mary said regretfully. "They're nothing special. A bit shabby and sort of homemade looking. No denims, nothing like that. And not dressy, neither. Like it might be a sort of uniform, only — I don't know how to put it."

There was a pause. She wondered if they believed her. She didn't care about Mr. Potts, but she wanted very much to convince Miss Timpson that she was telling the truth.

"What about their ages? Are they elderly?" Edward Potts asked at last.

"No. Come to think of it, they're mostly young. Not kids, I don't mean, but not as old as my dad. Oh, and I forgot to tell you. They've all got red ears."

"Mostly young. And quiet. Possibly in uniform. Nothing special about them, except for their red ears. Mary, it's cold for September. There's been a bitter wind. Lots of people have red ears. What makes you think these people are ghosts?"

"What else can they be? Anyway, I seen 'em summer and winter and they always have red ears. At least," she added fairly, "they do when the light's behind 'em."

"Like the ears of white rabbits?"

"Of course not," Mary said scornfully. "They haven't got rabbits' ears. They got ordinary ears, like us."

"Mr. Potts meant the color, the way the light shines through the blood," Miss Timpson explained.

Mr. Potts was writing in his notebook again, leaving a smear of cream on the page. Mary, squinting past the teapot at the upside-down writing, made out the words, "Red ears. White rabbits. Do ghosts have blood?"

"You say they don't talk? Not even to one another?" he asked next.

"I dunno," she said, frowning. "Not that I've noticed. They're usually on their own. They *can* talk, though. At least, the man with the dog can. He spoke to me yesterday. He knows my name. Look out the window! Oh, he's gone. He was there a minute ago, by that lamppost."

Both Miss Timpson and Edward Potts stared through the café window and across the road to where a solitary lamppost stood in the gathering dusk. Nobody was near it. Not a shadow marred its cool circle of light.

"No one there now." Edward Potts said.

"There you are then!" Mary cried. "If he was a real person, he wouldn't have vanished. I saw him plain, long nose, red ears, and his raggy dog and all. That proves they're ghosts, don't it?"

"No, Mary, I'm afraid it doesn't," Miss Timpson said gently. "It could mean that you're imagining it."

"I'm not! I'm not!" she shouted.

"Have another cake," Mr. Potts said soothingly. "Try one of those; I can recommend them."

"You don't believe me, do you?" Mary cried.

She looked very young. The light behind her

made her hair appear dark, except for a fiery halo around the edges. Her mouth drooped and her big black eyes stared at Edward sadly, without hope.

"The girl in the book!" he exclaimed. "That's it! That's who you remind me of. The girl in the book."

10

Mary could think of only one book at the moment — the book her mother had sold to the man in the secondhand bookshop — who in turn had sold to a man with a beard. She stared at Edward Potts, and he smiled back at her through his curly brown beard. "It was you! *You* bought my mum's book from that old bookshop."

"Do you mean Pepper's in Exton Street?"

"Yeah. She had no right to sell it. It's mine. It's all about me. You gotta give it back. I'll pay you. I'll give you what you gave for it — only you may have to wait for the money. How much was it?"

"Two pounds, but —"

"I'll give you one pound now and one next week. There, I can't be fairer than that. Where is it?" She saw him glance down at the briefcase on the floor by his chair. "It's in there, isn't it?"

Mr. Potts licked the cream off his fingers.

"Don't get so excited. I'm not sure we're talking about the same book. I haven't had time yet to read the one I bought, but it can't possibly be about you. It was printed at the end of the last century, long before you were born —"

"You said it had my photo in it!"

"Not *your* photograph. A photograph of someone who looks like you."

"Lemme see! Please!"

He hesitated, made somehow uneasy by her agitation. What on earth could be in the book to make her look so eager and so fearful? He said slowly, "Mr. Pepper said that the lady he bought it from —"

"That's my mum."

"Your mother then. He said she had told him it was all about her great-grandmother. Not her daughter, her great-grandmother. Are you sure the book is yours and not your mother's?" he asked.

"Yes, it's mine!" Mary had convinced herself of this. Why else would her mother have hidden it from her and lied about it, if it wasn't about her and the ghosts she saw? Her mother had always been odd about her ghosts, shifty, evasive, just as she had been about the black box. They must be connected.

She saw Mr. Potts was looking at her doubtfully and repeated, "It is mine."

"Yet you seem to know so little about it," Miss Timpson said, sounding puzzled. "Haven't you read it. Haven't you already seen the photograph?"

"I was only five when Dad gave it to me." Mary invented quickly. "I didn't read so good then. Mum said it was about my ghosts and would give me nightmares, so she hid it. She must've forgotten it was mine. She's always selling things or giving them away to charities. Tidying up, she calls it."

They both laughed.

"Then it seems only fair that you should have it back," Miss Timpson said, believing her.

Edward bent down, and opening his briefcase, brought out a slim volume in a shabby mottled green cover. Mary put out her hand to take it from him, but he held it out of her reach, saying, "Don't snatch! All in good time. Remember it's still mine. You haven't paid for it yet. And I'm not sure I'm selling. Let's have a look."

The title was in thin gold letters. *"True Encounters with the Supernatural,"* he read, "collected by J. D. Worple. Well, it is about ghosts," he said, smiling at her. "Don't snatch! You'll tear it, and then none of us will be able to read it. Try and be patient. Let's see." He ran his finger down the table of contents, muttering under his breath, "The Dragon of Chinatown, Mrs. Browne's Red Petticoats, The Islington Choirboy, The Clapham

Cab Horse, The Werewolf of Highgate Wood, Mary Coram's Other World — Mary Coram! That was her name! Page seventy-five." He began leafing through the book, while Mary and Miss Timpson watched him impatiently.

"Mary Coram," Miss Timpson murmured. "Does the name Coram mean anything to you, Mary?"

"No, Miss."

"What was your mother's maiden name?"

"Murphy. Bridget Murphy."

"Here she is," Mr Potts said, turning the book toward them so that they could see the photograph, but keeping hold of it with one hand. "Mary Coram. 1887."

They stared down at it and the girl seemed to stare back. Her eyes, black and sad and frightened, were fringed, like Mary Frewin's, with thick lashes. Her mouth was the same shape, the top lip arched, the lower lip full.

"She doesn't look a bit like me," Mary protested. "She's much too old. She must be at least twenty. And what a strange dress."

"I think it's some sort of uniform," Miss Timpson said. "She *is* like you, Mary, the shape of the face, even the way her hair grows off her forehead. Strange. You know, I doubt if she's more than fifteen or sixteen. Having her hair put up makes her look older. Poor child, doesn't she look unhappy."

"A complete drip," Mary muttered. "Let's hear what they say about her, then."

"I think I'd better just read through it first," Edward Potts said, "in case it contains something unsuitable for young girls to hear." He laughed at the howls of protest that greeted this. "All right. Here goes, and if you both have nightmares tonight, don't blame me. Don't say I didn't warn you."

Freda Timpson felt suddenly uneasy, but it was too late to stop him. Leaning forward, Edward Potts began to read in a low, clear voice.

11

" 'There is no doubt that the tone of morality among servant-maids in the metropolis is low,' " Mr. Potts read out. He stopped, glanced quickly at Mary, and said, "We don't need this introduction —"

"Yes we do!" Mary cried. "We need it all. I don't care if she was a servant. I don't care if she was a thief. It don't bother me. Go on."

He hesitated, glancing down to the end of the paragraph. "All right. Here goes. 'Maidservants in good families have an opportunity of copying their mistress's way of dressing and making themselves attractive to men of a higher class, only to find themselves abandoned when they are with child. It may be that this is just such a case, and the strange story Mary Coram tells is simply a pack of lies, as her mistress claims. However, I report it so that you may judge for yourselves.

" 'The known facts are these. Mary Coram was a

maid-of-all-work for a good family in Islington. From all accounts, she was a simple, ignorant, uneducated little body, as strong physically as a donkey, and thoroughly competent to perform her arduous duties, for which she received eight pounds annually, including her board and lodging —' "

"Only eight pounds?" Mary asked.

"Yes."

"For a whole year?"

"Yes. Remember, this is over a hundred years ago."

"They didn't have to call her a donkey, though," Mary said. "That's rude."

"Shall I go on?"

"Yes. Sorry. I won't interrupt no more."

" 'On 3rd September 1884,' " Mr. Potts continued, " 'she was sent on an errand from which she did not return. Her mistress, after waiting a few days during which time no trace could be found of the girl, took on another servant in her place.

" 'Two years later, on 16th November, Mary Coram appeared unexpectedly, coming to the kitchen door of the house in a confused state. It was obvious that she was expecting a child shortly. Naturally she was turned away, first by the servants and then, when she would not go, by the mistress of the house. For some days she wandered about the streets, crying and calling for "the Captain," though when people asked his name and to what regiment he belonged, she was unable or unwilling to say.

" 'Eventually, the Reverend Henry Field found her lying in the doorway of his church, half-frozen and in great distress, being near her time. He took pity on her and had her taken to the Home for Penitent Females in White Lion Street. Her baby was born the following day, Friday, 21st November 1887.

" 'The Reverend Henry Field, knowing I was interested in stories of supernatural experiences for this book, wrote to me and suggested that I should see her and hear her story.

" ' "You may be wasting your valuable time," he wrote, "for I cannot vouch for the truth of what she says, and it is an incredible tale. Yet I would be glad if you would see her and judge for yourself. There is something about the poor creature that is oddly convincing." '

" 'I agreed to see her, though I held no great hopes of finding anything of use to me. An opportunity was made for me to question her at the Home. I was shown into the Matron's room, and the girl was brought in to me, supported by an older woman without whose help she would have been unable to walk. She looked ill and faint, but the Matron assured me the girl was both able and willing to talk to me — especially since she was told I was bringing the new portable camera to take her likeness.

" 'What follows is an account of my interview with Mary Coram. I have used her own words, wherever possible. At times she became excited and would start weeping hysterically, which made her difficult to follow. I commenced by asking about her early life.

"I come from the Foundling Hospital, sir. They took me in when I was a baby and kept me till I was fourteen, when they put me to service with Lady Haberton. I was sad to leave my friends, but they said I was lucky to have so good a place, sir."

"Did you agree with them?"

"I don't know what you mean, sir."

"Never mind. Tell me, where did you meet your young man? Did he come to the house?"

"No, sir, missus didn't permit no followers."

"Where did you meet him?"

"Well, sir, I don't rightly know. Cook sent me out to fetch her some oil of cloves, she having the toothache bad. I was in Red Lion Street when I

come over peculiar. There was some rough boys crowding me. I held Cook's money tight and ran away. Then there was this bright light blinded me, and it was like everything was coming to pieces. I saw a head, sir, floating past like a moon with red ears, a head all by itself, sir, shouting at me. I think I screamed, sir, and then I fell.

"When I could see again, I was sitting on the grass in a field.

"No, sir, I don't know where it was. I thought I did but it wasn't the same. There was the old tree in the field — I know that tree. They taught me to write my name, sir, at the orphanage and I cut it into the tree so I wouldn't forget and I got a beating for it. Well, sir, there was my name, Mary Coram, so it must have been the same tree, but there was no orphanage there, just fields and a blackened ruin. I was afraid, sir, and I began to cry.

"Then my sweetheart came up — well, he wasn't my sweetheart then, just a stranger, and he was kind to me. He asked me a lot of questions, sir, like you. No, I don't remember exactly. He spoke funny. I did not understand what he said, except where I come from and what was my name, which I told him, and he told me his.

"What was it? It was foreign, sir. I couldn't get my tongue to it. He laughed and said to call him

Vop, but it seemed disrespectful, sir, so I called him Cap'n.

"He's a naval gentleman, sir, not a common seaman but an officer. He was dressed very strange. They all were, sir. He said they were waiting for their ship to come. I asked him where from would it come, and he said, well, it sounded like the sky, sir."

"The island of Skye, do you mean?"

"That must be it, sir. It was just that I never heard of such a place and I thought he meant . . . well, up there, sir.

"He took me back to his camp, and they crowded around me and talked foreign. Yes, there were others there. Mostly men. There were some women and boys, but not many, and not young children. No babies. They were kind to me, but at first I was not easy. I didn't like it that they spoke foreign. My sweetheart could speak English a bit, and so could the man with the dog. They asked me to teach the others. I am no teacher, sir, not being clever, but they laughed and said won't I try, so I did. I felt better having work to do there. I was happy, sir. I never remember being so happy before.

"My sweetheart married me. He did, sir. They all says it's a lie and I'm a wicked deceitful girl, but I'm not. It's true what I'm telling you. I swear

to God, sir. I wish I could go back there with my
baby. I know they would take me in, but I can't
find the way. I can't find the way back."

" 'Here Mary Coram became overcome by weeping and coughing, and I thought it better to leave further questioning until she was stronger. She did not want me to go. She clung to my hands and kept saying, "Don't let them take my baby away." She appeared to be frightened that they would give her baby son to the Foundling Hospital and she would never see him again. Telling her I would come back the next day to see what could be done for her, I left.

" 'As it happened, it was a week before I was able to return to the Home, by which time Mary Coram had gone. She had left two days ago, saying she was going to find her husband. She had wanted to take her baby with her, but was persuaded to leave him, as she was not yet strong enough to carry him and might do him an injury. They promised they would keep him there until she came back to collect him, but I think that was only to keep her quiet. By the time I came, the child was already at the Foundling Hospital and the young mother had disappeared.

" 'I made some inquiries after her, being sorry

for the girl and wishing I had come back as I had promised, not that I could have done anything. I did not believe her story at this time. These girls like to claim they have husbands. And yet there was something about her. I could not forget her sad white face and pleading eyes. She must have been a striking girl when well with that mass of heavy red hair. Even ill and bedraggled as she was, people remembered her, though this may have been because of the way she behaved. They told me she staggered down the streets like someone drunk, crying and coughing and stopping people to ask if they'd seen a foreign captain. Some street boys ran after her, mocking at her and yelping like dogs around her heels. It was from one of these boys, Tom Pewter by name, that I obtained the following account of her disappearance.

" 'He said, "We thought she'd been at the bottle the way she was mewling and moping, so we followed her. We didn't mean no harm. She went down Red Lion Street, sir, calling for the Cap'n all the way. No, sir, we didn't know no captain, but we joined in calling Cap'n, meaning to help her. Then there was this funny bright light everywhere, and a crackling noise like when you step on thin ice. Hands came out of the air, just hands, sir, nothing else. They took hold of the mad girl and pulled her along. She was laughing and crying, sir, and — and she vanished into thin air before my eyes. I saw it, sir. I saw her go. Bit by bit. First her hands, arms, head. . . . The last I saw of her was a curl of her red hair blowing and a corner of her dark skirt. I swear it's God's truth, sir, every word."

" 'Mary Coram was never seen again.' "

12

"They got her!" Mary said. "They took her away with them!" Her eyes were wild and bright, and she grabbed hold of Miss Timpson's arm. "Don't let him take me!"

"Don't let who?"

"Him! The man with the dog."

They all turned to look out of the window. It was darker outside now and a thin rain was falling. Beneath the solitary lamppost, the wet pavement shone like the moon, cold and empty.

"He isn't there," Mary said. She was trembling.

I wish I'd never told Edward, Miss Timpson thought. I wish he'd never got hold of that wretched book. We were going to help Mary, but we've only made her more upset. She glanced at Edward appealingly, but he was reading the book again and didn't notice.

"Lemme have a look," Mary said. "What else does it say?"

"There isn't much more. Here, see for yourself." Edward pushed the book toward Mary, and she bent over it, holding her hands over her ears to shut out any interruptions.

"What happened to the baby?" Miss Timpson asked Edward.

"He stayed at the Foundling Hospital," Edward told her. "The journalist left them some money for him and a copy of this book, to be given to him when he went out into the world, so he would have something to remember his mother by."

"Poor boy! It's hardly a comforting story."

"Oh, I don't know. He'd have been glad to find his mother loved him and had intended to come back for him. And who knows, he might've been proud to have his name printed in a book. I imagine they taught him to read at the Foundling Hospital. I wonder what they called him."

"Kit Coram," Mary said, looking up. "That's what it says here. Short for Christopher. I got an uncle called Christopher, but he can't see ghosts. Not like the other Mary and me."

"There's nothing there about ghosts, Mary," Edward Potts told her. "Look at the title: *Mary Coram's Other World*. That's what it's about, an alternative world. Not a word about ghosts."

"There is! There. Red ears, see? She's seen them, too. We are alike, her and me." She turned back to the photograph of Mary Coram and they all stared down at it. "Do you think I'll disappear too? I bet I do."

"Of course you won't, Mary," Miss Timpson said gently, frowning at Edward for introducing alternative worlds into the poor child's brain. "You mustn't be frightened anymore. If there's one thing this book proves it's that your ghosts are all in your imagination —"

"What!"

"Don't you see, Mary? When your father gave the book to you for your birthday, he must've read some of the stories to you, especially the one about your great-great-grandmother, Mary Coram. And your mother was right. It frightened you. It frightened you so badly that you hid the memory away, but you never quite forgot. The floating head, the red ears, they're just the things that would stick in a child's mind." She smiled at Mary and added, "I expect that's when you started seeing your 'funny people,' wasn't it?"

"No, it wasn't. I always seen them. I seen them in my pram," Mary muttered stubbornly. She'd never looked more like the photograph in the book, the sad black eyes, the drooping mouth.

Miss Timpson smiled and shook her head,

saying that it was a long time ago to remember exactly. "I'm sure I'm right, and it was this story that has always troubled your imagination. You agree with me, don't you, Edward?"

"Yes, it sounds very possible," he said in the hearty voice grown-ups use to reassure children. "It does seem to explain everything. So, you see, Mary, you needn't worry anymore."

They thought she would be happy to have her ghosts explained away. She was furious. Seeing ghosts was her one talent, her gift. She wasn't clever at anything else. Take her ghosts away and what was she? Just the girl at the bottom of the class.

Later that evening, Mary told Nonny and Isobel what had happened.

"They think I'm mad!" she said. "*She* does, anyway. You should've heard her. She wants me to see someone 'who's trained in helping people sort things out.' I know what that means. A nutcracker, that's what. A shrink. And he agreed with her. Whatever she said, he agreed with her. But he winked at me, so I dunno what he really thinks. When she went to the ladies' room, I asked him what he meant by another world, did he mean heaven? And he laughed and said no. He was talking about alternative worlds. I didn't really understand what he meant, but she came back, so we couldn't talk anymore."

They were in Nonny's tiny room, the three of them sitting cross-legged on his bed. His parents were out and his older brothers were in the sitting-room with their friends. Occasional bursts of laughter and loud music reached them through the closed door.

"I like him," Mary went on. "He said it was fascinating how my great-great-grandma's story matched mine — you know, the red ears and the floating head she saw. I told you my ghosts had red ears, didn't I, Isobel? And you laughed at me."

"And now you're telling me your great-great-grandmother married a ghost and had a ghost's baby, and I'm not supposed to laugh? That'd make you part ghost yourself, Mary. Which part? Your arm? Your leg? Your middle?"

She began to poke Mary in the ribs, and Mary dissolved into unwilling laughter. But she was still angry. She hated being tickled. It gave her the same helpless feeling she had when people refused to believe in her ghosts.

I'll tell Mum. *She'll* believe me, she decided. She knows I don't tell lies. Well, only now and then, and she says she can always tell. She'll help me convince them.

But her mother had no desire to convince anybody of anything. Her mother seemed only too glad to accept Miss Timpson's explanation.

"I was wrong about her," she said. "She must be cleverer than I thought, in spite of not teaching you your grammar. It's obvious she knows all about children, even if she hasn't got any of her own. Imagination, that's the trouble. Imagination's all very well in its place, but kids overdo it. In the end they can't tell what's true and what's false. Take you and your ghosts. I wouldn't be surprised if it didn't all start off with those damp patches up there." She pointed to the corner of the ceiling.

They were sitting side by side on the sofa in front of the television. Her mother had turned the sound off when Mary came in. On the screen the actors opened and shut their mouths soundlessly like ghosts. Mary dragged her gaze away from them and looked up at the ceiling.

"Mum, I've seen the book."

"What book?" Mrs. Frewin asked. But she knew. She knew all right. Mary could tell that just by looking at her.

"The book you kept locked up in that black box. The book you sold to that bookshop man and he sold to Mr. Potts."

"Mr. Potts?"

"He's Miss Timpson's boyfriend, another teacher, and he read us the part about Mary Coram —"

"He had no right to!"

"Yes, he had. It's his, Mum. He bought it for two pounds. You sold our family history, our heirloom what ought to've come down to me, for two pounds. If he wanted to, he could show it all over the school, and everybody will know my great-great-grandmother married a ghost."

"It was one pound, that's all I got!" her mother protested. "I didn't do it for the money. I did it because I knew it would upset you. None of it's true. Your great-great-grandmother didn't marry anyone, the poor child. She just said she did because she wanted to be respectable. She was frightened they'd turn her out. You don't know how cruel people could be in those days —"

"Yes, I do. They called her a donkey and paid her next to nothing. And when she was in trouble, they turned her out and she'd have died, only a clergyman come and took her to the Home where she had her baby. Do you know what the baby was called, Mum? Kit Coram."

"I know. He was my grandfather."

"I suppose he died before I was born. Did he have red hair like me?"

"Maybe. I don't remember."

"Did he ever say anything about his mother? Did he ever go looking for her? Mum? Mum, why don't you answer?"

Mrs. Frewin sighed. "I suppose you might as well know, dear. Your great-grandfather never forgot his mother. Gran told me once it was like he was haunted by the story in the book. He was always going back to the Foundling Hospital and to the little street where she disappeared, asking around everywhere, trying to trace the boys who'd said they'd seen her vanish. It was no good her telling him that the boys would make up any story you pleased for a penny. Of course, they wouldn't be boys any longer, they'd be grown men. He never told her if he found any of them or what they said. But one day, it was a Sunday afternoon, he said he had to go out. She'd wanted him to take her and the children to the fair, but he went out by himself. He seemed excited, she said. He kissed her and told her he wouldn't be late. 'I hope I'll have something to tell you when I come back,' he said. But he never came back at all. She never saw him again."

Mary stared at her, "You mean he just disappeared?"

"I don't know where he went, love. Maybe he was murdered and robbed. Maybe he fell into the canal. Maybe he went off with another woman, though my gran wouldn't hold with that."

"Or perhaps he just vanished into the air, bit by bit, like his mother," Mary said.

Mrs. Frewin put her arms around Mary and shook her gently. "That's just a story, love. A story in a book. Something somebody made up to amuse children, like rabbits in waistcoats and Father Christmas, something we grow out of when we grow up —"

"But Mum, the book said they were true! *True Encounters with the Supernatural*, that's what it was called. In gold letters!"

Her mother laughed and told her the color of the letters was no guarantee of honesty. "Your great-great-grandma made it all up because she was frightened, poor girl, and who could blame her for that."

I don't believe she made it up, Mary thought. I believe it was all true, every word of it. I believe she married her captain, and I'm not surprised that she was happier living with the ghosts or whatever they are than she'd ever been before. I think she found her way back to them, and that was why the boy heard her laughing and crying. And I bet that's where Kit Coram's gone. I'm glad he looked for her. I hope he found her. There must be another world somewhere — *and I'm going to find it*.

13

In the morning, Nonny got up early as he always did on Saturdays and tiptoed out of the bedroom so that he would not wake his brothers. He liked being alone in the kitchen while his family slept. No radios screaming out different programs. No Dad singing out of tune in his bath. No Mum and Auntie Vic yelling to each other from different rooms. Sitting on the stool and munching a jam sandwich, he planned his day.

At nine o'clock the doorbell rang. When he opened the door, he found Isobel outside. He sighed. His plans hadn't included her.

"I've got to talk to you," she said. She seemed agitated. She'd been chewing the ends of her hair into damp spikes, always a bad sign.

"All right," he whispered. "I'll come out."

Shutting the door quietly behind him, he led the way to the top of the stairway beside the lifts. They sat down side by side on the dusty top step, resting their elbows on their knees.

"What's the trouble?" he asked.

"It's Mary. She's crazier than ever. She called around last night, after she'd spoken to her mum, and said she was going this morning to look for the place where her great-great- — however many greats it is — grandmother disappeared. *And* her great-grandfather. He disappeared too, or so she claims her mother had told her. It's a lot of nonsense, of course. I don't really believe a word of it, but ... Nonny, supposing Mary vanishes? Think how awful I'll feel. D'you think I should've said I'd go with her?"

"Did she ask you to?"

"Yes."

"You mean you refused?"

"Well, it was so silly. She gets on my nerves sometimes, her and her stupid ghosts. Do you know what she says now? She says they may not be ghosts at all but a sort of alternative people, like God was practicing for us. That's why some of them are just bits, as if He was trying out an arm or a leg on a spare piece of paper. Yeah, I know. It's crazy. But that's what she said."

"Where's she going to look for them?"

"Coram's Fields."

"*Coram's* Fields? You mean, like in Mary Coram?"

"Yes. She found it on the map just above Red Lion Street where the Foundling Hospital should've been. Colored green and marked Coram's Fields."

"It must be a park, I suppose. Or a cemetery. Yeah, I bet that's it. A great place for ghosts. Great-great-grandma's in the cold, cold ground. What's she planning to do when she gets there?"

"I asked her, but all she'd say was, 'Come with me. I want a witness. If I vanish, tell them what happened and say I'll come back if I can.' What shall we do, Nonny?"

"We'll go with her, of course," he said firmly.

Jimmy Harding was a Bad-Dog Boy, newly joined and renamed by them Peke, because of his snub nose and bulging brown eyes. He ran to tell Pitbull his news, hoping to gain favor.

"Spooky Loonie and her friends are going off on a ghost-hunt this morning," he said, skidding to a halt in front of Pitbull, who stood with the other members of the gang in their favorite corner by the garages.

"Who says so?"

"Isobel, that's the blonde one with the long hair.

She told her mum and she told Mrs. Carver on the ninth floor and she told my mum who told my brother Kevin and he told me."

"Where they going on this ghost-hunt?"

"To Coram's Fields, that's what my brother said."

"Where's that?"

"Dunno."

"Dummy!" Pitbull said. "Yer should of found out." He looked across at Rottweiler. "Wot d'yer think? We could foller them. Might have a bitta fun. Jump out at 'em and make 'em shriek."

Rottweiler shrugged. "They're only stupid kids. Not worth bothering about." He was growing out of the Bad-Dog Boys. He didn't much care for Pitbull, whose feet stank. "Please yourself, however," he said, and walked away, taking his friends with him.

The younger boys looked at Pitbull whose pudding face went a dull red.

"They're scared," he said, when Rottweiler was safely out of earshot. "Remember how they ran when Spooky Loonie seen a ghost in the elevator?"

"Yeah," the boys said. They had all run, but they preferred to forget this. Only the one they called Boxer remembered. He too was getting tired of the gang. However, when they decided to follow Mary and her friends to Coram's Fields, he went with them.

The last people to set out for Coram's Fields were Freda Timpson and Edward Potts. It was Edward's idea. He rang her up after breakfast and suggested that she should come with him. "It's a beautiful day," he told her. "Much warmer than yesterday. We can have a picnic. Would you like that?"

"Yes, I would," Freda agreed.

She wanted to see Edward again, not only because she liked him, but because she was worried about Mary. It would be nice to hear Edward tell her again that she worried too much, as he had done when she was a practice teacher at his school. "Of course you'll pass your exams," he'd said, and he'd been right. Now she wanted him to tell her, "Of course Mary Frewin will be all right. Why shouldn't she be? Don't worry."

There was something very comforting about Edward. He was always so sure of himself. He might be clumsy. He might spill things and knock them over and trip over his own feet, but he knew where he was going.

"I'd love to come with you," she said now.

"Where are you thinking of going? Somewhere in the country?"

"Coram's Fields. It's in the city," he told her apologetically, "where the old Foundling Hospital was. I thought it might be built over with office blocks, but it's colored green on the map. Must be a park or a public garden. Probably full of late roses. I'll pick one for you if there's nobody looking."

"But why do you want to go there? What do you expect to find?" she asked.

"I don't know. A plaque to say it was the site of the Foundling Hospital. Trees, a bench for us to sit on if the grass is too wet, the scent of roses in the sun. . . . And who knows? Perhaps the sound of a young girl laughing and crying as she runs into the arms of her ghost husband? I'd just like to see it, to get a feel of the place. Aren't you curious, Freda?"

Now was the time to tell him that ghosts left her cold. She did not believe in them. Nor alternative worlds either. She only worried about Mary because the child saw things that did not exist, hallucinations that interfered with her schoolwork and overshadowed her life. However, she didn't want to argue with Edward. She liked him too much, even if what Mary said was true and he was as fickle as the weather. What did it matter, anyway?

She had no intention of falling in love with him. None whatsoever.

So she offered to make the sandwiches for their picnic and began cutting bread and butter cheerfully, pushing her worries to the back of her mind. I'll go and see Mary's parents sometime, she thought. There's no hurry. It's not as if she's in any danger. Next week will do.

It never occurred to her that next week would be too late.

14

Coram's Fields was neither a cemetery nor a park. It was a place for children, part playground with seesaws and a jungle gym, and part city farmyard with cockerels strutting and crowing in the bright sunlight. From somewhere in the background, Mary could hear the complaining bleat of sheep. Behind high-wire fences at the rear, boys were playing football.

She stared through the railings. She wasn't certain what she had expected, but it wasn't this. This open sunlit place was not a place for apparitions. There weren't many children yet; perhaps it was too early. Most of the ones she could see were small and plump and healthy. Here and there a solitary parent sat on a bench in the sun. None of them had red ears.

Isobel was standing next to her, reading a large notice. "No adults unless accompanied by a child," she announced. "No dogs, no glass bottles, no bicycles. Doesn't say anything about ghosts."

"I can't see any," Mary said, pretending a disappointment that she did not feel. "I haven't seen any all week."

She had started off determined to prove to the world that she had really seen ghosts. She was not mad. She'd follow in her great-great-grandma's footsteps and find out the truth, even if she had to disappear to do so.

But with each step of the way, she'd begun to change her mind. Supposing she couldn't find her way back? What about poor Mum and Dad? They'd never get over it. Mum got hysterical if she was only half an hour late.

"Let's go home," she said.

"We've only just got here," Nonny pointed out. "We might as well go in and explore. Might be interesting."

"What about *them*?" Mary asked.

They turned and looked down the street. A few yards away Pitbull stood with his gang of Bad-Dog Boys. They had lain in wait for them by the garages at Cloudsley Towers and followed them all the way here. Every time Mary looked around, she had seen them ducking out of sight, around corners or into doorways. They were hopeless at it. They couldn't have been more obvious if they had marched down the middle of the street carrying banners. Once Pitbull had tried to hide behind a short woman carrying a shopping bag and she had turned on him, threatening him with the police if he so much as laid a finger on her bag. Isobel and Mary had laughed. It had maddened Pitbull, who would probably have given up otherwise, not being fond of long walks.

Now he stood in the open, sweaty and furious, glaring at them. Some of his gang had slipped away when they got the chance. Even those who'd remained loyal to him looked tired and dispirited. Boxer was still there, standing a little apart.

"I don't like the look of them," Nonny said.

"Who would?" Mary asked.

Isobel hushed her nervously.

"Don't drive him too far," Nonny warned. "He might forget about my brothers. He's got an ugly temper. Let's go in. We should be safe enough there."

A collection of small children were now blocking the narrow gate into the playground, while a tall woman in green counted them. "One, two, three — where's Annie? Oh, there she is. Get in line, dear. Now where was I?"

The Bad-Dog Boys were closing in. Mary refused to look around, but she could hear the soft padding of their feet on the pavement behind her.

One of them giggled. Now they were beginning to chant softly under their breath: "Spooky Loonie Mary Frewin, we're gonna get you, gonna get you."

The woman who had just shepherded the last small child through the gate looked back and said sharply, "What's going on? Are these boys friends of yours?"

"Yeah, we're all good friends," Pitbull said. "Ain't we, dears?"

He pulled Isobel's hair gently to remind her she'd better agree with him. She shrieked and jerked away from him, leaving a few shining hairs in his thick fingers. He grabbed for her again, but Mary put her foot in his way so that he tripped, arms flailing. While he was still off balance, Nonny pushed him from behind. He fell heavily against Peke and they both sat down hard on the pavement.

"Stop that!" the tall woman shouted. "What do you think you're doing?"

They were running, that's what they were doing. Isobel and Nonny and Mary, running as fast as they could. Isobel ran in a blind panic, with no thought of where she was going, relying on her long legs to outrun their enemies. Nonny, though his legs were much shorter, was nearly as fast. Mary, the smallest and youngest, could not keep up.

Behind them, she could hear the baying of the Bad-Dog Boys getting closer. They were running now beside a building caged in scaffolding. Ahead of them, the scaffolding jutted out to straddle the pavement, and wooden barriers had been placed on either side to form a tunnel for pedestrians and roofed with green netting to protect their heads from falling debris.

Isobel raced straight into it, the gloomy light from above giving her flying hair and long pale legs a greenish tinge, so that she looked like some strange sea creature. Nonny and Mary followed her, feeling uneasy as the shadows closed around them and the peopled world was shut out. It felt like a trap, even though they could see the bright opening at the other end.

Halfway there, Isobel stopped so abruptly that Nonny bumped into her.

"What's the matter?" Mary called "Why —"

Then she saw what they had seen, the heavy figure silhouetted against the light ahead of them, unmistakably Pitbull. He must have raced along the road outside the tunnel and was now waiting like a dog outside a rabbit hole. "Gotcha!" he cried, while behind them the rest of the gang roared into the tunnel like a disorderly train.

The words from the book echoed in Mary's head. *"There were some rough boys crowding me...."*

She saw an opening on her right. "Nonny! Isobel! Here!" she shouted, and ran into the building site.

It was like stepping into an iron forest. The poles of the scaffolding grew up like tall trees, breaking up the sunlight into small shining fragments on the cluttered floor. Everywhere there were dim shapes, unidentifiable in the poor light, a wheelbarrow, some sort of machine half covered by a tarpaulin, a high pile of dusty bundles.

"Hey, you kids! You're not allowed in here!" an angry man's voice shouted.

Mary stumbled on through the patchy darkness, ignoring the voices, trying to find somewhere safe to hide. There was a rattle above her head, and something struck the ground near her, raising a cloud of dust.

"Get those kids out of here before they get hurt!" someone yelled.

Suddenly a glaring light dazzled her eyes. She saw the black poles tilt and lurch around her like falling trees. A wolflike dog with a humped back ran past her and vanished. A tall, thin shadow slipped after it and was gone.

"Mary!" a boy's voice called.

She tried to look back, but everything was cracking up into fragments, as if the world was a glass jigsaw that was coming to pieces. She heard someone screaming, "Mary! Mary!" Then she fell into the dark.

Edward Potts, walking with Freda Timpson towards Coram's Fields, was nearly knocked over by a gang of boys bursting out from behind the fences surrounding a building site.

"Hey, steady on!" he protested, but in vain. The boys were already across the road, knocking against the chairs and tables set out on the pavement opposite. "They seem in a hurry," he said dryly. "What's going on in there? There seems to be an argument. Let's go and see."

They went into the tunnel and found, standing in one of the entrances to the building site, Nonny and Isobel arguing with three men in hard hats. Another boy they did not at first recognize was standing nearby and weeping.

"If she's in there, we'll find her," one of the workman was saying. "We'll find her all the quicker if you let us get on with it. I've already told you —"

"What's the trouble?" Edward asked, coming up to them.

"Are you in charge of these children, sir?" one of the men asked, turning to him with relief. "If so, I wish you'd explain to them that nobody, absolutely nobody, not even the prime minister, is allowed in here without a hard hat. Look," he added, turning to the children. "You don't want me to lose my job, do you? We'll find your little friend for you and bring her back to you, safe and sound." He looked back at Edward and said, "There's a café across the road. You could wait there."

"Can't I help?"

"I'm sorry, sir. It's strictly against regulations for any unauthorized person—"

Miss Timpson left them to argue and turned to Isobel. "It's Mary, isn't it? You've lost Mary."

"She ran in there. We saw her, didn't we, Nonny? She called for us to follow. We were being chased by the Bad-Dog Boys — *his* lot," she pointed at the weeping boy. He tried to speak, but his mouth twitched and shook, and the words would not come.

"I've heard about your gang," Miss Timpson said. "You rush about trying to frighten smaller kids and old ladies. Did you all follow her into the building site?"

"We're not members of the gang," Nonny protested. "Boxer is, not us. The others took off. We tried to follow Mary; she'd called for us! But that foreman stopped us. He held me and Isobel, one in each hand, and then *he* slipped by. It wasn't fair. We are her friends, but he won't let us look for her —"

"They have strict rules about keeping people out," Edward said, coming up behind them. "I suppose I can see the point. Come on, let's go to that café. I don't know about you, but I can do with something to eat."

They sat at one of the outside tables and ordered tea and Coke and assorted cookies. "Don't let him have any," Isobel said spitefully, pointing at the Bad-Dog Boy, who was still crying.

"Why, what's he done?" Edward asked, not having heard.

"Nothing!" Boxer cried, his voice shrill. "I didn't mean no harm. I wanted to help her. I saw her duck into the building site, but the others didn't notice. It was dark in the tunnel, see, after the sun outside. I didn't tell them. I like Mary. I wasn't going to sneak up on her. I didn't mean her no harm."

Freda Timpson felt relieved. It was nothing to do with the supernatural. Just a gang of bullies teasing younger kids. Mary would be found soon, safe and well.

"There, don't cry," she said kindly. "You can have a cookie. And we must remember to save some for Mary —"

He began to cry again. "She's gone," he mumbled through his tears. "I saw her running through the scaffolding. I called out to her. Then there was this funny bright light everywhere and a crackling noise like when you step on thin ice. I saw her vanish. Bit by bit. Her hands, her arms, her head. . . . It was *awful*! The last I saw was her red hair like a stain in the air. Like a bloodstain! Then . . . then she was gone."

She comforted him, though she felt in need of comfort herself. For his story bore a frighteningly close resemblance to the account of the disappearance of Mary Coram, given by the street boy who'd chased her all those years ago.

It seemed like hours before the foreman came to join them. The sun had gone behind clouds. The bright day was over. They could tell at once from his face that Mary had not been found.

"No luck, I'm afraid. We've searched every corner. We've been up on every platform, and there's no sign of her." He dragged an empty chair over to their table and sat down heavily. "The men are having another look, but I don't see how we could have missed her. Don't look so worried, Miss. She probably slipped out before we started searching and has gone straight home."

"She's vanished!" Boxer said. "She's gone forever!"

15

There was a stink. That was the first thing Mary noticed. A stink of scorched metal and something else, something sharp and chemical. It prickled her nose.

No, that was the grass, she was lying on grass. It was so close to her eyes that it was out of focus, and she had taken the stems for the bars of a cage.

She sat up and looked around in amazement. She was in some sort of rough field. . . .

It had happened! All of it, the bright light and the world coming to pieces and then grass in a field. She was there, in the other world, where her great-great-grandma had gone all those years ago. There should be an old tree with a name carved on it. Mary Coram . . ."

There were trees all right, a whole forest full of them, their tops visible above a tall fence. This was a ramshackle affair, made out of rough wooden poles about seven feet high and six feet apart, with the gaps between them filled by an untidy mixture of piled stones, rusty metal, old bricks, and brush-wood, the whole lot threaded through by strands of glinting barbed wire.

Behind her the ground sloped down into a wide, roughly circular depression, in the center of which was the strangest ruin she had ever seen. Twisted girders and loops of an oily-looking plastic reared up into the sky, like the bones and guts of an exploded brontosaurus. Only bigger. Much bigger. From this blackened skeleton, tatters of a reflect-ing metallic substance hung, glittering in the sun-light. These stirred in the wind, confusing the eyes, so that it looked at times as if thin blue flames washed over the wreckage and leapt in glinting sparks from one broken girder to another.

There was no one in sight. There was only the rough field, the strange ruin, and the ramshackle fence. No houses. No sound of traffic. Nothing.

"Nonny! Isobel!" she cried.

Silence. Then in the distance, from somewhere behind the ruin, a dog barked.

"Is anybody there?" she called.

A man's voice shouted something, but she could not make out the words. The dog barked again and then yelped shrilly, as if in pain.

"I'm coming!" she shouted. "Wait for me!"

She began running over the grass, caught her foot in some sort of crack, and fell. Picking herself up, she went on more carefully. The field was treacherous, the long grass hiding a network of wide cracks, some deep enough to break a leg in.

The smell was stronger here, and she could hear sparks fizz with a noise like a wet finger on a hot iron. The whole ruined edifice seemed to twitch as if it had fleas, the rusty iron supports shifting like the legs of an animal tired of waiting. At times light flickered over it like flames and then the sparks flew. At other times everything was black and immobile against the sky. It was almost as if there were somebody inside it, switching it on and off.

"Where are you?" she shouted. But there was no answer. Even the dog was quiet.

She wanted to sit down and cry, but it wasn't raining. Her father had always joked about her being his brave little soldier. "Soldiers don't waste time crying when they're in trouble," he'd told her many times. "They find a way out of the mess they're in and save their tears for a rainy day."

"Why a rainy day?"

"It won't matter then. Everyone has wet cheeks when it rains," he'd said.

It was not raining now. That was all you could say for the day. Mary bit her lip and blinked. Through the tears in her eyes, she saw the ruin shimmer with its deceptive fire.

"I hate it here!" she shouted. "I hate this horrible world and everything in it."

There was a roaring sound, and she thought she felt the earth move under her feet. In a panic, she turned and raced toward the fence, leaping and stumbling over the half-concealed cracks, terrified that at any moment they might open up and swallow her.

But she reached the fence safely, and looking back, saw the ruin standing quietly under an unclouded sky. Close to it, the field twitched, like a coverlet over a restless sleeper. Long ripples ran through the grass like waves, dying out some way from where she stood.

An earthquake? An illusion? She did not know. Her instinct was to hide. She walked along the ramshackle fence until she found a gap wide enough to let her through into the woods.

The moment the green canopy of leaves closed over her head, she felt safer. The wood was ordinary and familiar, a wood of oak and silver birch and holly trees, like Highgate Woods where her mother used to take her when she was small, except that it was wilder, and there was no sound

114

of children's voices. No squirrels scampered up the trees. No birds sang.

But she had heard a man shout, she reminded herself, and the bark of a dog. She wasn't the only living creature in this uncomfortable world. She hadn't had her lunch, that was the trouble. She'd feel better when she'd eaten. She sat down by an oak tree and unfastened the backpack from her shoulders. At least she wouldn't go hungry. She had *all* their sandwiches. How lucky she'd offered to carry them. She had expected Nonny to say, "No, no. Give them to me, Mary. I'll take them." But he hadn't. Perhaps he hadn't wanted to come with her to Coram's Fields. . . .

The leaves rustled suddenly. A large wolflike dog ran out of the bushes, sat down in front of her, and fixed his eyes on her sandwich. She knew that dog. She recognized the rough coat and the humped shoulders and the yellow teeth.

A man and a dog, *this* dog — oh, no!

"Go away!" she said.

It looked up at her and then back at her sandwich. Saliva hung from its mouth in silvery ribbons.

"Oh well, at least you're company." She broke a piece off her sandwich and threw it to the dog. It caught it neatly, swallowed it down with one gulp, and looked back at her hopefully.

"Where's your master?" she asked.

The dog could not answer, of course. All it could do was eat her sandwiches and wag its tail when she spoke to it. She looked at it thoughtfully. When it had run past her into the bright light, someone else had followed, a tall, thin figure who might have been its master. She had not seen him clearly enough to tell. Did she want him to be here, the man who had haunted her in Islington, always behind her with this dog, the sound of footsteps and the clinking of its chain?

Might be better than nobody . . . might be worse. The man had frightened her. She didn't know why.

She shared a second sandwich and a piece of cake with the dog, then put the rest back in her canvas bag. Mustn't eat too much. Didn't know how long the food had to last.

The dog got to its feet and growled softly.

"Hey!" she began, indignant by what she took to be its ingratitude. Then she saw that it was not growling at her. It was staring into the woods, its ears pricked and its lips pulled back from its teeth in a snarl. Its hackles had risen, making it look more humpbacked than ever.

"What is it?" she whispered nervously.

Then she heard a voice in the distance, a man's voice calling, "Mary! Mary Frewin!"

The dog growled again under its breath. Mary sat silent, not answering, not moving, frightened.

The voice called again, "Calabal! Calabal! Vor en tun? Calabal!"

The man was nearer now. She heard the sound of leaves rustling and crackling underfoot but could see no one. She turned to look at the dog again in time to see it crawling on its belly underneath the low branches of a nearby holly bush, wriggling its way in until it was out of sight. One thing was certain: the dog had no wish to be found.

Infected by its fear, Mary looked around for a hiding place, and seeing nothing better, climbed up into the branches of a nearby tree, hoping that whoever came would not think of looking up. From here, she could see through the heavy leaves, patches of the ground below, little clearings bright with the afternoon sunlight.

Into one of these came the man with the pointed nose. Though he was some distance away, she recognized him quite clearly. He stood, turning his head and gazing through the trees, but never once looking up into their branches. Sunlight filtered down on him and caught the edge of one of his scarlet ears.

"Calabal! Calabal!" he called angrily. "Vor en tun, bahla ruff!"

Not a leaf stirred in the holly bush where the

dog was hiding. Mary remembered the yelp of pain she'd heard. Would a dog desert its master for one hard blow and a stranger's sandwich? Perhaps its life had been full of hard blows. Who could blame it if, finding itself free of its chain at last, it had run away.

The man was calling her again, his foreign voice now soft and ingratiating, "Mary! Mary Frewin! Where are you? Come, Mary Frewin. I can help you."

She stayed silent in her tree and watched the man walk away through the woods, until she could see him no longer. When the sound of his calling had died away, she waited a few minutes and then climbed down.

"Calabal?" she called softly.

No dog came. She peered into the prickly bush but could not see anything but leaves. Perhaps the dog had gone straight through and was now miles away. Why should it wait for her?

"Oh well," she muttered, and sighed. She hitched her bag over her shoulders and began walking, taking the opposite direction to that taken by the man with the pointed nose. At first she whistled as she went, to fill her head with cheerful music and keep gloomy thoughts out. Then it occurred to her that some creeping phantom might follow the sound, so she hurried on in silence, not turning her head for fear of what she might see.

After a moment, the holly bush started shaking and the dog crawled out. It shook itself and then started off after Mary. Having abandoned its cruel master, it was as lonely as she was. And it hoped for another sandwich.

16

Mary had no idea of the time. Her watch had stopped, and the heavy foliage overhead shut out the sun. She was surprised when she came out of the woods to find the misty September afternoon only just beginning to darken into twilight.

"Look, Calabal!" she said to the dog. "Aren't those houses over there? Dunno, though. They could be trees or clouds . . . difficult to see. There's a road, anyway. Let's cut across to it. There might be a bus."

She was glad that she had the dog to talk to, for the silence of the woods had got on her nerves, and she'd almost wished she hadn't hidden from the man with the pointed nose. The sound of a human voice, even if it was only her own, drowned out the dismal sighing of the wind. Calabal looked around when she spoke and wagged his tail in wordless friendship. She had never imagined a dog could be so great a comfort.

And she needed comfort. When they reached the road, she realized that no bus had driven on it for a hundred years or so. Plants grew up through its cracked and crumbling surface, thistles and ragged robin and brambles heavy with berries. She picked one and put it in her mouth but spat it out again: it had a bitter taste.

The town the road led to turned out to be a mere shell, desolate and destroyed. The dog, who at first had run ahead happily, now slunk back to her side, keeping so close that she could feel the warmth of his body against her leg. The town appeared empty. No light shone in any window, except that of the setting sun, shining red in the glassless holes of a ruined tower. The rubble spilled over onto the road, and everywhere there were deep cracks that showed no bottom, merely a blackness that might have gone on forever.

Here a row of houses was still standing, though the glass had gone from their windows and their doors hung loose. Oddly, they seemed vaguely familiar. There was a storefront she seemed to recognize. In the dim moonlight, she tried to make out the sign above the door. The paint was worn and smudged. Peffer's Secondhand Cooks.

"It don't make sense," she told the dog, as they walked on. "I'm tired. I can't think straight. I've never been here and yet — does it remind you of anything, Calabal? I keep imagining. . . . Look at that chimney — that doorway! Haven't you seen them before?"

The dog yelped shrilly and jumped sideways as if stung.

"What's the matter?"

Thinking Calabal might have stepped on some broken glass, Mary knelt down beside him and lifted his paw in her hand. Something small and sharp hit the center of her back. She cried out and fell forward behind a large slab of broken concrete. The dog ran away.

She lay on the ground. She'd been shot. At any moment she'd feel agonizing pain, and blood would gush out through the hole in her back, taking her life with it.

Nothing happened. No pain. No blood.

Perhaps she was already dead?

The dog came back, sniffed her, and licked her cheek. She sat up and looked over the concrete block. Immediately a small stone hit it and bounced off, followed by another one, and another.

Not bullets! Stones! Stones thrown by children!

"Stop that!" she shouted furiously. "Stop it or I'll set the dog on you!"

Three small gray figures ran like rats into an open doorway and disappeared. Calabal growled deep in his throat but made no attempt to chase them. Mary hesitated, wishing she hadn't shouted. She should have tried to make friends with the boys. Somewhere they must have fathers and mothers, brothers and sisters; perhaps a warm room with glass in its windows and supper cooking on the stove.

She could, of course, follow them into that dark, half-ruined house. They were only small kids, and she had Calabal to protect her. Not that Calabal seemed very brave. And there might be swarms of them in there. Small wasn't always beautiful. Think of piranhas, the little fish that could nibble you to death with their tiny teeth. Ugh!

She walked on quickly, taking the dog with her. It was getting darker. A lopsided moon had risen into the sky. Soon they would have to find somewhere to spend the night, to eat their last sandwiches and sleep.

They came to a small square, with an arched column on either side and a ruined building at the far end.

"Come on," Mary said. "Let's sit in that sort of

123

cloister and have our supper. We'll be out of the wind there, but not shut in. . . ."

Her voice trailed away. She could not explain why she was uneasy. She could not see anything, only moonlight and dust and stone. Calabal started whimpering softly under his breath, as if he were uneasy too.

She put her hand on his neck and whispered, "It's all right. There's nobody here."

As if to prove her a liar, figures stepped out of the arches and came toward her. She turned and saw they were behind her too. Calabal jerked from under her hand and ran. She tried to follow him, but tripped and fell onto her knees. When she looked up, she saw it was too late to run. She was completely surrounded.

There were about twenty of them, the people who stared down at her, some in their late teens or early twenties, some even younger. The moonlight was too dim for her to see the expression on their faces, but many of them carried sticks in their hands.

A tall young man, looming over her, spoke sharply in a foreign tongue.

"I d-dunno what you're saying," she stammered, frightened. "Can't you speak English?"

"I am speaking English," he said angrily, though with so heavy an accent that she could only just

124

make out the words. "I am a Crumb. All Crumbs speak English. It is our mother tongue. Who are you who speak English so badly?"

"I don't!" she protested, hurt that the way she spoke should be criticized in two worlds. "I am English. I'm the real thing. Not a ghost like the lot of you!"

To her surprise, several of them smiled at this; she could see the gleam of their teeth in the moonlight. Or perhaps they were getting ready to bite her?

"Where did you come from?" the young man asked, and when Mary looked at him blankly, repeated slowly and loudly, "Where . . . did . . . you . . . come . . . from?"

"Oh. From Islington. You know, it's near the city. I came here by accident. I'm sorry, but I'm lost. And I don't know the way back home. I suppose I couldn't stay the night here? It's getting dark now, and I'm so tired and hungry."

"What did she say?" he demanded. "Her tongue clatters like a runaway horse. And her accent is so terrible, I cannot understand a word."

"I was only —"

"Quiet!"

They began talking among themselves. Mary tried to listen, but they spoke so quickly that they might as well have been speaking Greek for all she could tell. It was getting dark and much colder.

She wrapped her arms around herself and shivered. The young man must have noticed because he turned to her and said slowly, "You are cold. We go in now. Stand still and be good, and we will not hurt you."

"Pardon?"

"Let me tell her, Keet," a pretty, plump young woman said. She turned to Mary, smiling. "Stand still, like this. Good. Now shut your eyes, like this."

There was no point arguing. Mary did as she was told. A bandage or scarf was tied over her eyes and her arms were held on either side by invisible people. Their hands were warm and rough and strong, which seemed odd for ghosts.

They don't want me to know the way to their hideout, she thought. They think I'm an enemy, a spy. They're as frightened as I am.

She was led forward over the rough ground, half carried up three steps, yanked upright when she stumbled.

"Stop!" a woman said. Her unseen captors spread her arms until her fingers touched a stone wall on her left and an iron rail on her right.

"It is a flight of narrow stone steps going down into the cellar. Do you understand?" the woman asked.

"I think so." Mary was beginning to get used to

their accent now. And the high voices of the women and children were easier to understand.

"Good," the woman said. "You must go down them by yourself, they are so narrow. Do not try to run away. We are in front and behind you. Walk carefully."

Holding tight to the rail, Mary walked down as she was bid. If they were there in the dark, they were very quiet. She could not hear their footsteps nor their breathing, only her own heart thumping in her ears.

I'm not frightened of ghosts, she told herself. If they really are ghosts. Wish I'd seen the color of their ears.

Suddenly, beneath the edge of the bandage covering her eyes, she saw a dim, uncertain yellow light. She stumbled over a step that wasn't there. Hands steadied her and pushed her forward over a flat floor. She heard the faint patter and rustle as people passed. Then the bandage was pulled off her head.

She stood, blinking. She was in a large window-less room, lit partly by firelight coming from the open doors of a large iron stove, and partly by a battered oil lamp that hung on a rusty chain from the ceiling. Its light shone down on her captors and she saw with surprise that their heads, like autumn trees, showed every shade of red from the palest shining orange to the deepest bronze of copper beeches. A small boy who stared at her with round black eyes might have been her brother, they were so alike. His red-gold hair curled in similar disorder about his ears — *scarlet ears!* Not pale pink like hers or dark brown like Nonny's, but thin, scarlet, semi-transparent ears. Ghost's ears.

So they really were ghosts. There'd probably been a war, she thought, remembering the ruined town and the wreck in the field, and they'd all died. Then why did they look frightened of her? Why did they all stand and gaze at her with silent amazement? It ought to be the other way around.

"Who d'you think you're staring at?" she asked boldly.

"Mary Crumb!" the young boy said, pale and wide-eyed. "I know you. You're the ghost of our great-great-grandmother. I've seen your statue in the graveyard. I've seen your picture in the history books. You're *dead*!"

17

She laughed. Nobody else did. The boy was obviously terrified of her. To her amazement, even the young men and women seemed to be nervous.

"That's stupid! How can I be anyone's great-great-grandmother? I'm only a kid."

"Time is unstable," said the young man they called Keet. "Everyone knows that."

"I don't. I don't know what you mean," Mary complained. "Anyway, I can't be a ghost, I'm not dead. I mean, am I? Do I look dead to you?" she asked, beginning to be frightened for they regarded her so strangely.

They did not answer.

"All right! So I'm not looking my best. But that's only because I'm cold and tired and hungry."

"Come over to the fire," Keet said. "Gally and Belois, bring her some bread and cheese and a cup of milk."

He led her toward the open stove. They were followed by several men of his own age and two tall stern young women who eyed Mary critically, frowned over the UP THE GUNNERS slogan on her sweatshirt, and raised their eyebrows at her striped football socks and grubby trainers. The others followed behind them, whispering and peeping, but keeping their distance.

The plump young woman, with frizzy orange hair, pushed forward a wooden chair and said, "Sit down, if you please."

Mary sat. The chair was hard. She'd rather have sat on the sheepskin rug on the floor but didn't want to argue. All she wanted to do was sleep. She wished they'd go away, but of course they didn't. They stood around her, talking in their strange foreign voices, asking her questions she could not understand. Her head began to spin. She put her hands over her ears and shut her eyes. For a moment, there was a sweet silence.

Then her hands were gently pulled away from her ears. She opened her eyes and saw a boy of about Nonny's age kneeling beside her. Although he was a heavily freckled white boy, he reminded her somehow of Nonny. His dark eyes were as bright and friendly, his wide smile as kind.

"Don't go to sleep yet," he said. "Look, here's some bread and cheese. Good cheese. Narkol

130

made it. At least, Narkol made the milk and I turned it into cheese." His voice was high and clear, and though he had an accent, he spoke slowly and she could understand every word.

"How can you make milk?"

"I can't," he said, laughing. "Narkol can. She's a goat. I'm in charge of our animals. Well, not the horses, just the goats and chickens and dogs. My name's Gally. What's yours?"

"I'm Mary."

"Mary," he repeated, and his eyes flickered. Behind his pleasant face, she could see the other faces, watching and waiting. Waiting for what? I'd better be careful what I say, she thought. He may seem like my first and only friend in this strange world, but he's one of them.

"You like dogs, don't you?" he went on.

"Not particularly," she said cautiously.

"But there was a dog with you. You were talking to him like an old friend."

"Oh, that dog. Yes, I liked him — though I don't know why. He's greedy and not very brave. He ate half my sandwiches and then ran away when you all came. But he's not mine."

"It was Calabal, wasn't it? I know him well. I used to look after him for Prosson sometimes before they — they went away. You're right about poor Calabal. He was always a timid dog. I thought Prosson was too hard with him. Have you known them long?" he asked.

The listeners stirred and drew nearer, as if her answer mattered to them, though she couldn't see why.

"I don't know who Prosson is. I've seen the dog before, with his master. His master frightened me. I dunno why. I'm not usually frightened of ghosts. But that one, he give me the creeps. He and the dog followed me through the streets —"

"Here in Izel?"

"No, back home. In Islington, where I live."

"Islington? I have not heard of it. Is it a village?"

"No," Mary said, laughing. "It's part of London."

"And London, what is that?"

She stared at him, frightened again, for he was not joking. Surely even a ghost would know what London was.

"London's the capital of England," she said.

"Who is this London she talks about?" Keet asked the boy. "Is it a man? I cannot understand her."

"I'll find out," Gally said, and turning to Mary, he asked, "This man who followed you, do you know his name?"

"No."

"What does he look like?"

"He's got a pointed nose and a chin like a fish's, and he's very tall and thin."

"That's Prosson!" Gally cried. "Keet, she has seen Prosson. He must be dead. She says he's a ghost."

Mary nodded. "Got red ears," she explained. "Like all of you."

"Everyone's got red ears!"

"Not bright red, they haven't," Mary said, and pushed her hair back to show him. They all clustered around her, staring and exclaiming.

"Nasty," the plump young woman said, shaking her head sympathetically. "I've never seen ears so pasty-white. You ought to be in bed, my dear. Keet, don't question her anymore tonight. She's exhausted. Leave it to the morning. It doesn't matter for now who she is. Look at her. Even if she isn't Mary Crumb, it's obvious she's one of us —"

"Except for her ears," he said.

"A bad case of anemia, that's all that is, poor child," the woman said, putting her arm around Mary. Mary, who was feeling dizzy, rested her head gratefully on the plump shoulder and shut her eyes. She heard Keet saying that they must find out about Prosson now. At once. Other people joined in, agreeing and disagreeing. Their voices merged into a low humming like the traffic in City Road. Mary fell asleep.

The plump young woman's name was Dafre. She and a tall, thin, freckled woman called Bibian carried Mary along the passage, with the young men following them, arguing, getting in the way.

"If you're not careful, you will make us drop her," Bibian said.

"I have already offered to carry her," Keet reminded her stiffly. "I am stronger than you. It will be easy for me."

"And easier for you to wake her up and ask her silly questions. The poor child's ill," Dafre said. "You yourself put me in charge of the sickroom. We are taking her there now, and I want no interference from you or anyone else."

"But Dafre, it's important. We must find out about Prosson. It can't wait. Supposing he's followed her here? She said something about him following her —"

"Back home, that's what she said. He followed her through the streets back home in Islington, wherever that is. You know what I think? I think she's from the other side. If Prosson is not dead as we thought, he may have found his way there at last. They're welcome to him. Let's hope he stays there."

"Amen to that," Keet muttered.

"Open the door, will you, please," Bibian said. "One thing is certain, she cannot be a ghost. She is surprisingly heavy for so thin a child."

"I know she is not a ghost. I never thought so for a moment," Keet told her stiffly, opening the sickroom door for them and following them inside. He looked around the empty room with its three narrow beds. "You are not leaving her here all alone? Without a guard? She could run off in the night."

"We will stay with her," Dafre told him. "Now leave us, all of you. Yes, you too, Keet. We must undress her and put her to bed."

The young men left reluctantly, saying they would be back, insisting that they must speak to the girl tonight — it was a matter of urgency.

"Later, later. Let us settle her first. She is ill, I think. Do you want to kill her with your questions? We'll tell you when she's ready."

They shut the door firmly and went back to Mary. She lay on the narrow bed, looking very small and delicate, the color of her skin nearly matching the woolen blankets, her lips and ears pale. Only her bright hair glowed like a fire on the pillow.

"She looks just like the paintings of Mary Crumb," Bibian said softly, gazing down at her. "Even to the color of her ears, did you notice?"

"Don't you start. We'll have all the young ones refusing to sleep tonight. She's very thin and cold. Get me a warm nightgown. Yes, that will do. You know, this child is no more than twelve, if that. See how flat her chest is. There is no way she can be the ghost of Mary Crumb, who was in her twenties when she died."

"Not ghost. I didn't say ghost. Supposing she *is* Mary Crumb, come back through the warp."

"How could she be? You forget, Mary Crumb didn't vanish, like the others. Mary Crumb died," Dafre said firmly. "Her tomb has been in the graveyard for a hundred years or so."

Bibian leaned forward and whispered, "But they say there are no bones in it. They say her coffin is empty."

"Who says?" Dafre asked sharply.

"Flak told me, for one, and Krono."

"How do they know? Have they dug her up? Have they looked?"

"They say Prosson told them before he too disappeared. He told them Mary Crumb had been seen on the other side. He told them he was going to fetch her back."

They both stared down at Mary uneasily. Then

Dafre said stoutly, "I don't believe it. Just because she looks like the portraits. So does Gilli. So does Kob. So do a lot of us. It's just a family likeness —" She broke off as Mary mumbled in her sleep.

"Great, great, great . . ."

"What's she saying?"

"Great, great-grandma . . ."

"Did you hear that? Did you hear, Dafre? She's telling us she is our great-great-grandma —"

"Too many," Mary mumbled. "Too many greats. Too many grandmas. One, two, buckle my shoe . . ."

"She's just talking nonsense," Dafre said.

"Shh! Listen . . ."

"Crumb, crumb," Mary muttered, turning restlessly. "Shouldn't eat biscuits in bed . . . too many crumbs — crumb, crumb, ker-rum — Coram! Mary Coram!" Her eyes opened wide. She looked at them for a moment and then said with great disappointment, "Oh, you're still here. I thought you were a dream, and I'd wake up safe in my own bed at home. I wish . . ." Her voice trailed away and her eyes shut.

"Poor child," Dafre said softly. "I too wish she was safe in her own bed, wherever that is. And whoever she is."

"She's Mary Crumb!" Bibian insisted. "She said the name just before she woke up. At least, I think she did. Her accent's so peculiar. . . . Prosson must have brought her back with him. He said he was going to.

"Why did he let her go, then?"

"Perhaps he lost her in the woods. Perhaps she ran away. She thinks he's a ghost, remember. She must be frightened of him."

"I hope she is," Dafre said. "She has reason to be."

18

At ten o'clock that night, Mrs. Frewin sat on the sofa in her sitting room, crying into the cup of tea that the policewoman had made her. Words babbled out of her in a watery rush.

"I always knew something like this would happen ever since she first told me she could see them. She's seen them since she was in her pram, you know. She used to call them the funny people, and I pretended I didn't know what she meant. But I knew all right. Not that I ever saw them myself, but my mother did and my Auntie Rose, only they grew out of it. I didn't tell Mary. I thought it might make her worse, knowing it was in the family. So I kept it from her, hoping she'd grow out of it like they did, and then she'd be safe. But that horrid man came —"

"What man?" the policewoman asked, seizing the one promising fact out of this flood.

"The horrid man up there," Mrs. Frewin said, pointing to the ceiling, "and his dog, see?"

"You mean he lives in the apartment above?"

"No, no, there isn't any apartment above. We're at the top. There's nothing above us," Mrs. Frewin told her, "only the sky."

"But I thought you said the man was up —"

"On the ceiling. There! Can't you see?" Mrs. Frewin cried, and burst into tears. Mr. Frewin took her into his arms and comforted her, looking over her head to say to the police, quite unnecessarily, "She's upset."

"Very understandable, sir," they said, though in fact they did not understand in the least. They had noticed the stains on the ceiling, as they noticed most things, having been trained to be observant, but they were just stains to them. They did not see in them, as Mrs. Frewin did, the shape of a man's face, and a dog with a humped back. If she'd told them about Mary Coram and the other world, they wouldn't have believed her. They would have thought worry over her missing daughter had addled her poor brains.

Freda Timpson and Edward Potts drove round the lamplit streets between Cloudsley Towers and Coram's Field. Every now and then, they stopped the car and got out to stand on the pavement and peer into the shadows and call her name.

"Mary! Mary! Mary!"

No answer.

"She's so young," Freda cried. "Anything could happen to her. If only we hadn't shown her that wretched book, she'd never have heard of Coram's Fields. She'd never have gone there. She'd never have run into the building site and — oh, Edward, it's all my fault."

"Not yours, mine," he said. He put his arm around her. The same lopsided moon shone down on them that had shone down on Mary in the town of Izel. Edward looked up at it and wondered if there could possibly be such a thing as an alternative world and what would happen to that poor child if she'd stumbled into one.

"Look, there's old Potty and Mary's teacher over there. Kissing," Isobel said with disgust. "*They* don't care about Mary. If you ask me, it was their fault for showing her that book. That's what set her off."

They were sitting in the back of the Richards's car, being driven by Nonny's big brothers. Mrs. Richards had persuaded Isobel's mother to let her go with them. "You can trust Seb and Tony to

141

look after them," she'd said. "They'll drive around, and if they see Mary, they'll bring her back. A long shot but at least they'll feel they're doing something to help. Better than staying at home and crying. And who knows? They might be the ones to find her. She wouldn't hide from them."

Mrs. Frayne, looking at her daughter's tear-stained face and pleading eyes, had agreed. "Just for an hour," she'd said.

They were on their way back now. They'd seen many people in the quiet streets and squares, some hurrying with their heads down as if afraid of what they might see, some strolling arm and arm, with eyes only for each other. But no Mary. Now Seb drew the car up beside the two teachers, rolled his window down, and asked them if they'd heard any news about her.

"I'm afraid not, Sebastian. We've been searching —" Edward said.

("So that's what he calls it," Isobel muttered to Nonny. "Does he really think he'll find Mary in Miss Timpson's ear?")

"— all over the place," Edward went on coldly, pretending he hadn't heard this. "But we haven't had any luck. She's probably staying with a friend and has forgotten to let anyone know." He looked at the two in the back. "Try not to worry too much about Mary," he said gently. "I'm sure she'll turn up safe and sound."

Nonny and Isobel did not answer.

When they had gone, Edward sighed. What else could he have said? Why did spoken comfort always sounds so hollow? Because one tells lies, he thought, kind lies. Everything will be all right, one says, as if one were God.

In the ruined town of Izel, Mary slept peacefully, dreaming she was back home. Dafre and Bibian took turns staying awake and watching over her. Once, during Dafre's watch, Keet came in, wanting to wake Mary.

"She can go back to sleep afterward," he said. "I must talk to her about Prosson right away. It is important. She said she saw him on the other side. He must be alive, then. I don't believe in ghosts. How do we know he hasn't followed her back here? After all, his dog came with her. Prosson may be outside now —"

"Then we'd better keep quiet and hope he'll go away," Dafre said, shooing him out of the room. "No point in running in the dark. We'd only fall into a crack and break our necks. Let Gally question her in the morning —"

"Gally? He's only a boy."

"She's more likely to talk freely with him than with you, Keet. He's got an easy way about him, and let's face it, you haven't. You bark at people, and besides, she cannot understand your accent."

"It's she who's got a bad accent, not me," Keet said indignantly. "You're always criticizing me, Dafre. If you're not satisfied with me as leader —"

"Oh, go to bed, Keet," Dafre said, laughing. "You're a very good leader in most ways. I didn't mean to insult you. But you frighten that poor child in there. Come morning, I'll have Gally and Belois give her breakfast and see what they can do. Go to bed."

He turned on his heel and walked quickly away. Dafre went back to Mary, shutting the door quietly behind her. Bibian was asleep on one of the spare beds, but Dafre could not rest. She wished the door had a key she could turn. She wished twigs outside would not scratch against the grating of the cellar like fingers trying to get in.

19

It was still dark when Mary woke up. On a table opposite her bed, a candle flickered in a saucer, agitating the shadows that crowded around her; but they were only shadows. There was nobody there. She sat up. While she had slept, someone had undressed her and put her into a shapeless woolen garment, clean but worn. She could not see her own clothes anywhere. No slippers. No shoes. A cold stone floor to cross to a door that was probably locked —

But just as she thought this, the door opened and a tall, thin girl came in, carrying two pairs of leather sandals in one hand and some clothes in the other.

"Here you are," she said. "Try these on. I hope they fit. You have got small feet, haven't you?"

"What time is it?" Mary asked, bewildered, for

145

it seemed to her it must still be night and this girl no more than a dream.

"Time is unstable," the girl said, putting the clothes down on the bed. "Even your own quite primitive scientists discovered that time is only relative. He should have come here — what was his name, by the way?"

"Do you mean Mr. Rogers?" Mary asked.

"Rogers? No, I have never heard of a Mr. Rogers."

"He teaches science at our school. He's primitive all right. All big and hairy like a gorilla, and scratches his chest. The boys call him the Missing Link."

The girl laughed. "No, I think the name I wanted was Einstein, but I may have got it wrong. Keet would know. These clothes are clean and nearly new. I will turn my back if you are modest. Then we can have breakfast."

"Breakfast? But it's the middle of the night!"

"No, we lost the middle of the night. There was a small quake —"

"An earthquake!"

"No, no, a timequake. It was nothing much, no need to look alarmed. We only lost an hour or two."

"What do you mean?" Mary asked, totally confused.

146

"I mean it's morning now. Time for you to get up. Are you dressed?"

"Nearly. It's so dark," Mary complained, scrambling into the woolen shirt and baggy trousers the girl had provided her with.

"Only because we're in the cellar. Hurry up. It's a beautiful day outside. Sun shining. Birds singing. Everyone is happy because there is no sign of Prosson anywhere. He can't have followed you after all. Even if he is not dead, he must be still on the other side."

Mary was silent, bending down to fasten the sandals. Prosson was what they called the man with the pointed nose. She'd forgotten to tell them that she had seen him in the woods yesterday, calling for her and Calabal. She had been so sleepy. Perhaps she should tell the girl now? But if she did, the girl would tell the others and they would crowd around her and question her in their difficult voices, all talking together so that she would not be able to understand a word. And she was hungry! She wanted her breakfast. She wanted to get out of this dark cellar.

So straightening up, she just said, "I'm ready now."

The girl picked up the saucer with the candle and led the way out into a narrow passage. They passed two other dark rooms and then came to the large room Mary remembered from the night before. It was empty. Daylight flooded down the stone steps in the corner, making her blink.

"Where is everybody?" she asked.

"Working. Dafre told us to let you sleep late."

"Dafre?"

"Fat. Frizzy hair. Pretty and kind," the girl told her. "She looked after you last night. Come on!"

She blew out the candle and led the way up the stairs into a roofless and ruined house, bright with sunlight and carpeted with flowering weeds and rubble and dust.

"Be careful where you step," the girl said. "There are cracks. . . . Follow me."

She took Mary through the house into what must once have been its kitchen, for there was an earthenware sink under the glassless window and an old-fashioned solid fuel stove along one wall, on which a large black kettle was steaming. A woman was sitting by a wooden table shelling peas.

"Oh, there you are, Belois," the woman said. "Gally thought you were never coming. He's waiting for you in the garden. Go and join him. Your eggs will be getting cold." She stared hard at Mary. "So you are the girl from the other side. Tell me, do you have kitchens like this over there? Do you have sinks that are cracked and leaking, and

148

taps that have never worked and weeds growing through the floor?"

"Um — not where I live," Mary admitted, thinking of their small kitchen, a fraction the size of this one, yet fitted with absolutely everything Mum needed, and most of it still working. Nowhere to sit down in the sun and shell peas, but who needed to, when you could buy them in packets and keep them in the fridge? True, the fridge was a bit temperamental, and there was mold on the bathroom walls, but you couldn't expect perfection.

"Mind you, it isn't so good for everyone," she said, thinking of the people who were not lucky enough to have a nice apartment at the top of Cloudsley Towers, people who had no home at all, who slept in doorways and cardboard boxes and died young. "Poor devils, pray God we never come to it," her mother often said. "Someone ought to do something." Mum was always saying that. Someone ought to do something.

But when she tried to say this, the woman interrupted her, saying impatiently, "It can't be worse than here. If you really are Mary Crumb, as they claim, the sooner you lead us over to your own world the better."

"But I'm not her. I can't —" Mary began, but

the girl hustled her out of the door before she could explain that she was not Mary Crumb nor Mary Coram or whoever they kept mistaking her for. She was Mary Frewin and she couldn't lead anyone to her own world because she didn't know the way back.

"Don't take any notice of her," Belois said, when they were outside in a tangled green garden. "She's always complaining. It's not so bad here. Or it wouldn't be, if it wasn't for the quakes. Here's Gally. Do you remember him? Yes, I see you do, and like him too. Your face has gone all soft and smiling. Everyone likes Gally. Even I do, and I am his twin sister. My name's Belois, by the way."

They did not look like twins. Gally was small and sturdy, with deep bronze hair curling around a heavily freckled face. Belois was tall and thin, with long pale orange hair. Her eyes were much lighter than her brother's, being almost amber while his were black. They were both wearing loose woolen shirts and baggy trousers, like the ones she had been given.

"I've laid breakfast over here, on what used to be the lawn," Gally told them. "I had to roll on the grass to flatten it, but it should make soft sitting."

He had spread a large cloth over the ground under an old apple tree. There was bread piled in

150

baskets, butter on a brown dish, honey in a pottery jar, six brown eggs arranged on a cabbage leaf, milk in a jug, and three pottery mugs.

"I hope the eggs will be all right," Gally said. "It is difficult to time them properly because time is so unstable here. You never know when you may gain or lose a minute or two —"

"Or a day or a week," Belois interrupted. "We lost our birthday last year. There was a bad quake, the worst for ages. People out that night said you could see the new moon shiver and shake, and then suddenly there it was, round as an orange in the sky, and all the leaves fallen from the trees. Nearly two months gone, as far as anyone could judge, and our birthday with it. Kob refused to give me the presents she had made for me, said she'd save it for next year, the mean wretch. I hope she loses all her birthdays —" She broke off, seeing Mary's face. "What is it? You look quite dumbfounded."

"I dunno what you mean," Mary confessed. "It don't make sense. How can you lose your birthday? We don't have earthquakes in England much, but I know all about them. We did them at school last term. It's to do with the earth's crust being on plates, and sometimes they bash into each other and crack, and things fall down —" She saw them

151

exchange amused glances and said defensively, "Well, I wasn't listening all the time. Maybe I missed a bit. But it was something like that."

"Yes, yes," Gally said soothingly. "A very vivid description. We have earthquakes, too. There was a terrible one here long ago, followed by a great fire. Nobody lives here now, except us and other runaways. They say it is too dangerous to rebuild. It is not so much the earthquakes — there hasn't been a bad one for many years. Not since before I was born. No, it is the timequakes that worry people. Don't you have them on your side?

"Don't think so. Mr. Rogers didn't say nothing about them. What are they?"

"I think I'll leave it to Belois to explain," Gally said, grinning. "Agriculture is more my line. Belois is the one who's good at physics."

Belois did not seem grateful for this praise, nor in any hurry to explain anything to Mary. She sucked a tail of her long orange hair, reminding Mary suddenly of Isobel. "How much do you know about physics?" she asked.

"Not very much."

"Do you understand all about quantum mechanics?"

"Um, no."

"Do you know what an electromagnetic field is?"

"Um, not exactly."

"What about a quark? You must know what a quark is?"

It sounded to Mary like the cry of a duck with a sore throat, but she just shook her head dismally.

"It is extremely difficult to explain timequakes to somebody who seems to know absolutely nothing about physics," Belois said complacently, sounding rather like a bird complaining that the worm can't bite back. "Well, I must do what I can. Let me see." She paused, then said very quickly, "Timequakes occur when you get a serious warp in the space-time and electromagnetic fields. The effects are increased when the warp is found near the boundary between two alternative worlds, such as we have here. Do you understand?"

"Mmm," Mary said doubtfully.

Belois gave the small, smug smile of someone who has got away with something. "What she means," Gally said, taking pity on Mary, "is that time is all messed up. We ought to move further away from the wreck. It's true most of our quakes are small here, but it gets on your nerves. It's very confusing, not knowing whether it's tomorrow or yesterday, and if the dogs have been fed or not. And the big quakes are horrid. They give you hallucinations and addle your brain. Makes it difficult to plan ahead, so people don't bother. Prosson used to say the uncertainty has sapped our initiative and we have become lazy. He was always shouting at us, but he wouldn't let us leave with the others. He called them fools. He said there was nowhere to go except into your world. He once told us we were trapped in the fifth field. I was only little then, and I thought he meant a field with grass and cows, so I asked if there wasn't a gate somewhere. He boxed my ears and called me an idiot."

"He tricked us. I'm glad he is dead," Belois said fiercely. She paused and added slowly, "But how can he be? You said you'd seen him. When was this?"

"I saw him yesterday in the woods —"

"In our woods!" Gally cried. "You mean, on this side?"

"Yes."

"Yesterday?"

"Yes. He was calling for —" She hesitated, wondering whether to admit that he had called for her by name. She didn't want them to think he was her friend.

"Calling for the dog? For Calabal?" Gally asked.

"Yes. Calabal was frightened and hid under a holly bush. I climbed up a tree and saw him pass below. He didn't look up. I watched him walk out of sight, still calling for his dog. I waited a long time, then I climbed down and went the other way. I dunno why. He's never done anything to hurt me. I could've asked him where I was, but — I don't like him. He's a bit creepy, isn't he?"

"He's deadly!" Belois cried. Her face had gone milk-white. "I must go and tell Keet. Gally, stay with her. Warn her about Prosson. Tell her how many of us died in the wreck. Tell her what happened there!"

20

Mary sat on the grass, with a piece of bread tilting in her hand and honey running unheeded down her fingers. Beside her, the dog Calabal sat and stared at the bread, his dark eyes reproachful when she ignored him. She was watching Gally move around the garden, poking the thick bushes with a stick, peering up into the trees.

"What are you looking for?" she asked.

"Just making certain he isn't here."

"Who?"

"Prosson. He's a sneaky creeping devil. It's always best to look in dark corners. . . ."

"Wouldn't Calabal have sussed him out?"

"Have what? Oh, do you mean sniffed him out? Yes, you're right, of course. He would have known. He'd be cowering with his tail between his legs, poor creature, if Prosson were anywhere near." Gally threw the stick down and came over

156

to sit beside the dog. Calabal flipped his tail politely, but did not remove his eyes from Mary's bread.

"You were right to hide from Prosson, Mary," Gally went on. "If you ever see him again, don't stop to talk. Don't listen to him — he can be a persuasive devil. Just run! Run like a hare. The man's wicked. He nearly killed me once."

"Why? What had you done?"

"Nothing. Oh, I don't suppose he *wanted* to kill me exactly. He just didn't care whether I died or not. He used us, just as he would use anything that came to hand to serve his purpose. I don't think he saw us as human. He drove us down to the wreck like sheep —"

"The wreck?"

"Yes. It's in the large field behind the woods."

"I've seen that!" Mary burst out. "At least I think I have. Do you mean that huge blackened thing that sometimes flickers with blue fire —"

"That's it. You must've seen it during a quake. The fire is only an optical illusion." Gally squatted down on the grass in front of her. "Some sort of electrical disturbance. It doesn't burn your feet. It just feels odd — like pins and needles —"

"What was it before it was wrecked?"

Gally shrugged. "Some people say it's the remains of an abandoned skyship. They say our people came originally from a place called Het Neptal, ages ago, before anyone can remember. But there are many different accounts; nobody agrees on anything."

"If it crashed, wouldn't everybody in it have been killed?" Mary asked, breaking off the crust on her bread and throwing it to Calabal.

"Not if they had escape-shuttles on board. My grandfather says there were two shuttles found in the woods, and that's where we got our electricity from, before the batteries ran out. But he is getting very old now. He might have dreamed it. My friends and I couldn't find them when we looked. And many people say it is all nonsense. They even claim the wreck is an unexploded weapon, aimed at us from your side, but Keet says you haven't the necessary technical knowledge to break through the barrier. He says you are rather a backward people."

"We're not!" Mary said indignantly. "You mustn't judge us all by me. I may not be very bright —"

"I think you are," he told her, lying in the long grass and smiling up at her. "Your brightness blinds me, Mary Crumb, to the colder charms of the girls at home. The way your hair burns gold in the sun — I forget how it goes on. It's from a poem written to Mary Crumb by her husband. We had to learn it at school." He smiled, watching her rather slyly from under his eyelashes. "It could have been written for you, Mary."

"No, it couldn't. For one thing my hair is red, not gold. And for another I'm not Mary Crumb. I'm glad her captain was nice to her, though. They were so horrid to her on our side. That is, if we're talking about the same Mary. Her name was Coram, not Crumb. C-O-R-A-M."

"That's right. Crumb," he agreed cheerfully. "Only you pronounce it so oddly."

"She was my great-great-grandmother," Mary told him haughtily. "If anyone knows how to pronounce it, I do."

"She was our great-great-grandmother, too. All we Crumbs are descended from her. And we pronounce it Crumb. If you're not *the* Mary Crumb, I suppose you must be just another cousin." He sounded somewhat disappointed, but Mary was delighted. She had so few relatives. No cousins at all except an old lady in Worthing. Now she had —

"How many Corams are there over here?"

"Oh, lots, but do not bother about them now —"

"Why are they all Corams? Didn't Mary take the Captain's name when they married? What was it, by the way?"

159

"Vophallomas Vopazakajez."

"Oh."

Gally laughed. "He was a Neptal. They all have names nobody can pronounce. He took her surname when they married. Now we are all Crumbs, whichever parent the name comes from."

"Is Prosson a Coram?"

"No, nor a Neptal. He's a Drowlian, one of the old people. Though he would like to be a Crumb. He resents us. He is always sneering at us, claiming we fancy ourselves an elite. There is nothing he loves more than to make us feel stupid. And yet he envies us. It was he who collected all us Crumbs together. He tricked our parents. He flattered them by praising us. We are supposed to be students in the Prosson Scientific and Technological College, given free board and lodging and tuition by the Council because of our exceptional talents. Father was so pleased and proud that Belois and I had been chosen. He did not know that all the young Crumbs had been chosen, and do you know why?"

"Because you are clever?"

"No. Because when we are young, many of us can see glimpses of the other side, of your world, Mary. I can myself, and so can Belois, though not often now and not clearly. Sometimes we can only see fragments of people —"

160

"That's how it is for me," Mary burst out excitedly. "I used to call them the funny people, but Isobel said they must be ghosts because nobody else could see them. They used to call me Spooky Loonie. They didn't really believe me. Even Isobel didn't. That's why I came over here. I wanted to prove I wasn't mad. I thought if I could bring something back to prove I'd been here, they'd have to believe me, see?"

She gestured with her hand and Calabal took the opportunity to remove the last of her bread neatly from between her fingers.

"Does it matter?" Gally asked lazily. "If you yourself know it's true, why worry what the rest of your world think?"

"Because I might be mad. Like the woman Isobel told me about who thought she was a teapot." She fumbled in her backpack and brought out a small camera. "Look what I've brought. I'm going to take photographs of everything —"

"Your film won't work," Gally told her. "Not if you've been through a quake. Sorry, Mary, all our films were ruined too. Nothing like that works here anymore."

"It wouldn't have done me much good, anyway. I don't know how to get back," Mary said sadly. She put her fingers against her mouth to steady it and tasted the sweet stickiness of the honey.

He stared at her. "Don't you remember the way you came?"

"No. Do you know, Gally? Can you show me? Please —"

But he was shaking his head. "Nobody knows," he told her. "Not anymore. They say that before the great earthquake and the fire, there was a way through. The split, they called it. It was difficult, they say, but not impossible. A few brave people went through and brought back books from your side, on your history and sciences, even some poetry. They were put in the Mary Crumb Museum in Camptown, which was lucky. All our other records were kept here. Look! You can see the top of the building over there, that thing poking up between those two trees. There!"

She looked where he was pointing and saw behind the vivid greenery a row of pointed gray ruins, like bad teeth masticating a mouthful of lettuce.

"That used to be our library. The tall one. All gone. Nothing left but stone and cinders. Puff! All our past vanished like smoke. Now no one can agree on anything, not even who we are. Me, I can't see it matters. I mean, here we are, sitting in the sun, with good food in our bellies. That's enough for me. But it worried Prosson. Prosson

162

used to have us digging in the ashes to see if we could find any scorched fragments of books or papers, but all we found were bones."

"Bones?"

"A lot of people died in the earthquake and the fire that followed it."

"Oh. Oh, I'm sorry," she said, horrified and awkward.

"It was a long time ago. Another age. Later they searched for the split, but never found it again. In the end they decided that it must have healed over, like a cut. Now most people have forgotten you could ever get through. Not Prosson, though. Prosson kept looking for it. I don't know why he was so interested. I suppose he thought the knowledge would give him power. He is very ambitious. That's why he wanted us Crumbs. He knew some of us could see people on the other side. He thought that must mean we could find the split, if we really tried. He was always saying that. "Try! You could find it if you really tried!"

"But even if you'd found it for him, could he have gone through? Can anyone get through?"

"Oh, yes. You don't have to be a Crumb for that, just brave. It was always dangerous, because of the quakes. Impossible without knowing the way. But if we'd found it for him, Prosson would

163

have gone. He didn't care about the risk. He was always brave." He stopped and looked at Mary unhappily. "I was younger then," he said. "He frightened me. I was terrified."

"He frightens me too," Mary told him.

"He used to take us down to the wreck, a few at a time," Gally went on. "Even though he knew how dangerous it was. Some never came back. He told us they had gone off to join their parents, but we didn't believe him. We knew they must be dead. People had died there before. Old people went there, hoping to be young again, young people looking for adventure, even children impatient to grow up . . . risking their lives even though they'd been warned of the danger. That's why the fence was built, to keep them out."

"I don't understand."

"They say the wreck is the very center of the warp — the time trap we call it. Time is all there; the past, the present, and the future, all muddled together like pieces of a jigsaw. A giant, three-dimensional jigsaw without a picture on the lid of the box. One false step may transform you instantly into an old man or a pile of bones. One false step and you may dwindle rapidly into a howling baby, or go screaming into the darkness before you were born. That's what we think happened to you, Mary

Crumb. You fell into the past a hundred years ago and vanished. And now you've been born again on the other side and have come back to help us."

"No," she said firmly. "I'm not Mary Coram. I'm me, Mary Frewin, and I can't help you. I'm only a kid. I can't even help myself."

There was a pause, and then Gally smiled and said, "Never mind. We'll just have to try and help each other."

"Did Prosson ever take you to the wreck?" she asked.

"Yes. Last summer. It had been raining. He lifted me onto a girder and it was wet. Slippery. He had a notebook in his hand, I noticed, and a pencil to mark down the way I went. He was making a map. I was not on the first page. He'd done it before with other boys. I wondered if he put a big cross where they fell to their deaths. I was so terrified, I could not move. I just stood there.

" 'Go on! Go on!' he shouted at me, himself standing safe enough on the grass. 'Walk, you little coward. Don't you want to be famous? Don't you want to go down in history as the boy who found his way through? Or died nobly in the attempt?'

" 'No, I don't!' I screamed, 'I don't care a pig's eye for your history! Let me down!'

"Keet was there. He leapt up, caught my hand,

and pulled me onto the grass beside him. Prosson knocked him down and threatened to kill him if he interfered again. Then he lifted me up onto the girder once more, standing on his toes to do so. I grabbed hold of the girder and swung at him, kicking him with my feet. He must have been off balance. He went sideways into the time trap. I heard him scream. I swear I didn't mean to kill him! I swear I didn't." He looked at Mary, his eyes wide with horror.

"I know, Gally," she said quickly. "Don't worry. Prosson didn't die. He's not a ghost; none of you is. I was wrong about you all. Mr. Potts (he's a teacher back home) said something about an alternative world, though I didn't know what he meant at the time. Still don't understand, come to think of it. But he must be right. This is all real, isn't it? This grass, the trees, the dog, and you. As for Prosson, I told you. He followed me back from my world. He keeps following me. I dunno why."

Gally gave a great sigh. "I never looked to see what happened to him," he said. "His scream! It's haunted me. I was so sure he'd seen his death coming. I jumped down off the girder and ran to Keet. 'Is he dead?' he asked, and I nodded. I could not speak. He took my hand and we ran. I could hear Calabal barking, but when I glanced back, he had gone. He must have jumped in after him. I wept for poor Calabal that night, but I never wept for Prosson. I told myself I was glad, glad he was dead. But often I hear his scream in my sleep."

"Poor Gally. But it's over now."

"We didn't go back to the college," Gally told her. "We were afraid people would blame us for his death. So we hid out here in the old town, and the other students joined us. We've been hiding out ever since. Keet sent a message to our parents, saying we were safe but not telling them where we were, in case they were questioned by the police in Camptown. I don't know if our tutors ever looked for us. The college is empty. Belois and I went to see one night, without telling Keet. There were no lamps in the windows, and the laboratory was covered with dust. I expect they all moved back to Camptown."

"Where is Camptown?"

"Not very far. I'd like to take you there and show you our great-great-grandmother's statue, and her gravestone in the cemetery, even if she doesn't lie beneath it. The Captain's grave is next to hers —"

"And their son Kit? Did he get here? He was my great-grandfather. Walked off one day and never came back —" She bit her lip. Would people at home say that of her? Walked off one day and never came back. . . .

"Don't look so sad!" Gally said, putting his hand on hers. "Think, if he hadn't come here, where would I be? He was my great-grandfather too. You can see his grave as well, if you like. But I'll have to ask Keet if it's safe for us to go. It can't matter now if they recognize me, but your face is too well known, Mary. I expect Prosson has gone there, and you don't want to run into him, do you?"

"Yes, I do," she said. She could believe Prosson was wicked. She had always been uneasy about him from the first time she'd heard his footsteps behind her in Islington and the clink of the dog's chain. But he was the only person she knew who'd been over to her side and back again. The only one who could tell her the way. And why should he refuse? "If I ask him politely, he might tell me how to get home," she explained.

"No!" Gally cried, exploding into alarm. "You must keep away from him! If he gets hold of you, he'll never let you go. He has plans for you —"

"For *me?*"

"Yes. He told everyone he'd go over to your world to fetch you back here —"

"*Me?*"

"Yes — well," he said, looking at her doubtfully. "He called you Mary Crumb —"

"I told you! I'm not Mary Crumb!"

"He won't believe you! He'll make you be her. You don't know what he's like. You better ask Keet. He knows. He'll tell you."

21

But it was three days before she saw Keet again, and then only from a distance. He had gone off with his friends on more important business, leaving Mary in Izel, without even a guard to watch her. Not that she thought of running away. Where would she have gone? She spent most of her time with Gally. Sitting lazily with a rabbit on her lap, she watched him milk the goats, half dozing, half listening to him talk. She still felt drained of energy, and though she asked him to show her the way to the wreck, she couldn't be bothered to argue when he refused.

"You don't want to go there. It's the worst possible place for you at the moment. Stay with us here until you're strong again. You know you get tired easily."

"I can't think why. You never let me do anything."

"Dafre says you have to rest until you've got over the quake. She'd skin me if she found you cleaning out the pigsty. Tell me more about your Islington while I finish these goats."

"No, you tell me about Izel," she said, and frowned suddenly, looking across the small paddock to the ruined buildings on the other side. "Izel Town — Islington. . . . Gally, it's funny. Lots of things here sort of remind me of home, only all wrong, like in a funhouse mirror."

"That's all it is," he said, soothingly. "A reflection. We're very near the edge here. You have to expect things to be a bit strange. You miss your home, don't you? Dafre tells me you call out, 'Dad! Dad!' in your sleep and cry —"

"Only when it rains," Mary said, but went on before Gally could ask her to explain. "Are you our future, Gally? Is Islington going to be ruined like this one day? I dunno what an alternative world is. I know it's not our past — I've done history at school. Is it our future?"

"No, no. You're thinking backward and forward in time." He paused. "You have to think sideways," he said.

But when she asked him what he meant, he shrugged. She had a feeling he didn't know either.

* * *

On the fourth day, when she and Gally and Belois were having lunch in the garden, Dafre came running out of the house. She smiled at Mary and said "Good. You are looking better now." She then forgot her, her head being too full of excitement to worry about Mary now. There was news! Splendid news! Arnesto and Kollos had come back! The new camp was established. There was to be a meeting in Camptown tonight to which everyone was invited.

"All of us who want to return with them must start packing," she said. "They want to leave before the new moon, no later, for fear of getting caught by the winter storms."

"How far is it?" Gally asked, his eyes shining.

He wants to go, Mary thought in dismay. They'll all go off and leave me.

"A long way, well over a hundred miles," Dafre told Gally. "Right out of range of the quakes, they say."

"What's the place like?"

"Rough, apparently. The ground needs clearing, but the soil is good. There is a river, spring water in the hills, and woods with plenty of trees for felling. Everyone is welcome, providing we can bring provisions to see us through the first winter and seeds for the spring planting. And as many animals as we can spare. You must come, Gally. You'll be needed to look after them —"

172

"And me?" asked Belois. "Will I be needed?"

"There will be work for everyone," Dafre said, looking a little uncertainly at her, "but perhaps not the work we would choose, not at first."

"You mean no need for scholars? For scientists? Just people to sow the fields and scrub the floors and brush the mud off the cows' bottoms?" Belois asked bitterly.

"Worse than that. We'll have to dig the fields before we can plant them and build the houses before we can scrub the floors," Dafre told her, laughing. "But come and hear what Kollos has to say about it before you decide not to go." She turned to lead the way from the garden, with Gally following too eagerly to notice that Mary still sat on the grass.

It was Belois who remembered her. The others had vanished into the house, but Belois turned and looked back across the tousled grass.

"Mary, you must come too," she said, holding out her hand. "Did you understand what Dafre said? About the new camp?"

"Yes." Mary was completely used to their accent now and had listened carefully. She steadied her voice and asked, trying not to let her dismay show, "Will you all go? What about Prosson?"

"I doubt if he'll want to come. He'll be furious at their success. I thought when the expedition set out that he hoped we'd never see them again."

"Why?"

"He's not a farmer. He wants to herd men, not sheep and cows. He does not like to get his hands dirty — except with blood. He doesn't mind a few killings. But the men who went are stronger than he is, and they despise him. He'll want to stop as many people going as he can." She smiled and added, walking slowly toward the house, "However, we're safe now. I don't know what he can do to harm us. His friends cannot accuse Gally and Keet of murdering him when he is still alive. We can come out of hiding at last. Kollos saw Prosson in Camptown, strutting around like a bedraggled peacock, talking to the crowds about Mary Crumb. I wonder what he was saying."

She turned and led the way into the house. The woman who had been sitting at the table had gone, and the kitchen was empty. Belois helped herself to a handful of peas from the iron pot and held them out to Mary. "Have some? Don't you like raw peas? I do. I'm always hungry." (She was indeed extremely thin, as tall and skinny as Isobel.) "I hope they have plenty of food."

"You and Gally, will you go?"

"Gally will want to. Did you see his face light up? I shan't be able to stop him. It's his idea of heaven. He'll build us a house with his own hands. It may be a bit crooked, but it'll be warm and dry." Belois sighed. "And I shall cook and wash his clothes and feed the chickens. Until my dear brother gets married, that is, and then what will I do?"

"Get married, too?" Mary suggested.

"I don't want to be a wife! I want to be a scientist!" Belois said furiously. "And what chance will I have of that in their new camp? There'll be no schools there, no colleges — just dirty pots and pans like these, and muddy fields and cabbages."

They went out of the house and into the cloistered square. Some way ahead of them they could see Gally and Dafre hurrying to catch up to a group of excited young men.

"Look at them," Belois said. "They can't wait."

"Do you have to go with them? Couldn't you come with me?" Mary asked hopefully, longing for a friend. Nonny and Isobel were so far away, and even Calabal had deserted her.

Belois turned and stared at her. *"You?"* she asked. "And where do you think you're going?"

"Home. I've got to go home. Poor Mum and Dad, they'll be frantic, thinking I'm dead or something. Come with me. There're plenty of schools on our side. You could stay with us. You'd have to share my room —" She stopped, not at all certain that Mum would welcome another girl to look after.

Belois was looking at her very oddly. "I thought

you told us that you did not know your way back to the other side?"

"I don't. There was this bright light — I couldn't see where I was going. But Prosson must know. He has been there and back again. I could ask him."

After a pause in which Belois dreamed of a new world, filled with schools and colleges, she sighed. "How could I leave Gally? He's my twin, my brother. And you must keep away from Prosson."

"Why? I bet he only followed me because I look like all of you. I bet he thought I knew the way over and hoped I'd lead him to it. Which I suppose I did," Mary admitted. "He ought to be grateful and tell me how to get back."

"He won't tell you a thing. Not Prosson. Not unless you have something to offer in return. Careful where you walk! There're cracks. Some of them are deep. Better keep close to me."

"Where are we going?" Mary asked.

"To Camptown. To the meeting."

"I'd better stay here. I might get lost —"

"It's a straight road all the way. Look!" Belois pointed.

They had left the square and were walking beside a wide ditch or canal, with muddy water at the bottom. Above them, she could see the backs of a terrace of dilapidated houses leaning against one another for support. She could not see anything that resembled a road.

"Where?" she asked suspiciously.

"*There!* Over that bridge," Belois pointed to a plank that spanned the ditch, "and straight on, where all the people are. Can't you see Gally?"

Mary could see Gally all right, jumping from boulder to boulder like a skittish mountain goat. She just hadn't realized that the rubble-strewn gap between the ruined buildings could possibly be regarded as a road.

"How far is it to Camptown?" she asked.

"Ten miles. An easy walk."

"Ten miles!"

"Yes. What is the matter with you? Are you afraid of a little walk? Or is it the plank?" Belois asked scornfully. "Perhaps you are afraid of falling into the water?"

"It looks dirty," Mary said crossly. "I'd probably catch something. Look, what's that moving in that rubbish down there! I bet it's a rat."

"You're scared!" Belois cried. She ran lightly across the plank and taunted Mary from the other side. "Stay where you are, if you like, Mary Who-ever-you-are. Though I'd better warn you, there are plenty of rats in town. Human rats as well as the four-footed kind. We're not the only people to hide out here. There are thieves and murderers and gangs of wild children who'd slit your throat for that bag you wear on your back —"

"There's nothing in it," Mary told her, beginning to edge nervously across the plank. "Only a few stale crumbs and my autograph book and my dad's camera. They can't have that! I gotta get it back before Dad notices it's gone —"

"You mean you stole it?" Belois asked, shocked.

"No, I didn't. I borrowed it," Mary said, flushing. "I'd have told him, but he was asleep. Besides, he'd have wanted to know where I was going, and if I'd told him, he'd have stopped me coming here." The plank wobbled under her feet, and she looked down and saw her own pale face reflected in the dirty water, like a leprous balloon. "I wish he had," she muttered. "I don't like it here."

"Hurry up!" Belois said.

Mary took another step. The plank shook more wildly. "I'm gonna fall!" she cried.

A tall man pushed past Belois and strode onto the plank as if it was as wide and steady as Westminster Bridge. He took Mary's hand and turning, pulled her after him onto the bank. The plank slipped away under their feet and splashed into the water behind them.

"So you are the girl everyone is talking about," the man said, looking down into her face. "They are wrong. You cannot be Mary Crumb after all.

Mary Crumb would not have been afraid. Mary Crumb was never afraid. She was a saint."

A small group of people had gathered behind the man. Mary saw Gally and Dafre among them, staring at her. They were all staring at her. She was suddenly very cross. "She wasn't no saint! She was just an ordinary girl. I read all about her. She was young and poor and people were horrid to her. I bet she felt cold and lost and frightened at times. Just like me."

"Just like you," the man repeated, smiling. Then his face became grave. "Stay with us, Mary. We'll keep you safe," he said.

Mary thanked him, but wished she had not heard an old woman's voice behind him mutter gloomily, "As safe as may be, poor creature."

22

The cart jolted over the road, leaving the ruined town behind. On either side there was rough grass, dotted with a few crooked trees and sprawling clumps of brambles. The only animal in sight was the slow gray horse between the shafts of the cart. Gally sat in the driver's seat and held the reins loosely, leaving the horse to pick its own way.

Apart from him, there were only women in the cart. Mary looked at them resentfully. They were all strangers to her. She was squeezed in between the tailboard and a fat old woman, whom everyone called Ma. Mary didn't like her. She was too bossy.

After the tall man had lifted Mary in, he had thrust an overlarge straw hat over her head, almost blinding her.

"Wear that," he'd said.

Mary threw the hat off, but he had walked away to join his friends without a backward glance.

"Who was that?" she asked.

"Kollos," the old woman said. She picked up the hat and pushed it down over Mary's bright hair again like someone extinguishing a candle. "Didn't you hear what he said? You're to keep it on."

With that she turned her back on Mary and began talking with her friends. The rattling of the cartwheels over the stony ground made it impossible to hear what they said. Mary, pushing the wretched hat up from her eyes, looked back over the tailboard and saw the walkers on the road behind, keeping up easily with the cart. She thought she saw Belois among them, but she could not be sure. She waved, but her movement made the hat slip down over her eyes again: she could not see if the girl waved back.

Most of Camptown was made of wood, endless small wooden bungalows, some painted white, some plain. Some were in rows, with fenced gardens separating them from the unmade roads; others just sat any which way on the ground as if a child's hand had dropped them and nobody had bothered to pick them up.

"Aren't there any shops?" Mary asked, peering out from under the brim of her hat. She was hungry. It seemed a long time since lunch.

There were stalls in the town square, the old woman told her, looking around. "We're nearly there. Keep hidden."

"Why?"

"Because Kollos said so."

"But why?"

"It's no good asking me," the old woman said. "I don't know. Just do what you're told."

The cart began to rattle and shake like a mad thing over cobbled streets. Now the buildings were higher, two stories or more, some of them made of stone. They came to a large square surrounded by large buildings. Mary could smell food, rich and spicy, and she saw a row of stalls on her right, on one of which someone was cooking something in a large iron pot.

"See that statue over there?" the old woman asked, nudging Mary. "That is the statue of Mary Crumb." She leaned back, lifted the brim of the straw hat, and peered doubtfully at Mary's face. "They say you're her. It's beyond me," she mumbled, shaking her head. "You're only a kid, aren't you? I don't understand all this time business. Doesn't make sense."

The cart stopped outside one of the large buildings. Two men came up and lowered the tailboard, holding out their hands to help them down. The old woman quickly pushed the hat down hard over

Mary's head, leaving her in the dark. She felt herself lifted up and placed on the cobbles. She could hear the cart creaking and Gally's voice shout, "Whoa back there! Mind out!" Something bumped into her and she blundered away, tugging at the hat, which had jammed painfully over her nose.

"What have we here?" a young voice inquired. "A walking toadstool?"

Hands began to spin her around and around as if she were a top. She dragged the hat off and saw a circle of whirling, grinning faces. She was surrounded by children. They were silent now, staring at her. Then the whisper began, "Mary Crumb, Mary Crumb, the old devil's right. He's brought her back."

"But she isn't with him," a small boy said. "If he brought her back, why isn't she with him?" He fixed Mary with a stern black stare. "Did you come with the old devil, Mary Crumb?" he asked.

"I dunno who you mean by the old devil, though I can guess. You're talking about Prosson, aren't you? Well, I didn't come with him and I'm not Mary Crumb. I'm Mary Frewin."

There was a general murmur — "What's she saying? Why does she talk so funny? Can you understand her?"

"I'm not Mary Crumb," Mary said, loudly and clearly.

"Yes, you are," the small boy told her, shaking his head disapprovingly. "You shouldn't tell lies. There's your statue over there. I'll show you." He took her hand and led her over the cobbles, followed by his companions.

A boy of about her age came up on her other side and demanded, "Why can't we go with Kollos to the new settlement? Why do you want us to stay here?"

"What d'you mean? What's it got to do with me?"

"Father said we could all go, and now he says we can't because Prosson's telling everyone *you* say we have to remain here. I don't want to stay here. I want to go to the new camp and build a new world—"

"Go, then!" Mary said, exasperated. "The sooner the better, I don't care. I told you. I've told everybody until I'm tired of saying it. I'm not Mary Crumb."

"Then why does it say you are?" the small boy asked, and pointed. A man moved out of her way and there was the statue in front of her. She gazed up at it.

So this is Mary Coram, she thought. This is my great-great-grandma.

The statue stood with both feet planted firmly on her pedestal, looking calmly over Mary's head.

In one hand she held a book and in the other a small bottle. What was in the bottle? Mary wondered.

Letters carved into the pedestal said MARY CORAM. FOUNDER OF SCHOOLS AND HOSPITALS. LIVED BRAVELY. DIED YOUNG.

Hospitals. Not gin in the bottle, then, but medicine. How did she have time to do so much when she died young? Mary remembered the description of Mary Coram in the green book — "a simple, ignorant, uneducated little body, as strong as a donkey." How could they have misjudged her so?

"Why didn't they put the date she died?" she asked.

The children shrugged. "Don't suppose they knew. There were terrible quakes in those days, teacher said, worse than now."

"You should know," said the young boy. "You were there."

"I wasn't!"

How could they mistake her for Mary Coram? The girl in the statue looked so confident. Nice, but tough. A good friend to have in a fight. It's true she was small and didn't look much older than Isobel. But she was not a child. She'd grown up since the days when she'd run through the streets of Islington, crying for her foreign captain.

"She doesn't look as if she ever cried," she said.

"If she'd had a dad, he wouldn't have had to keep telling her to be brave, I bet."

"You're wrong," they told her. "Of course Mary Crumb cried. It says so in the history books. She cried over the people who were killed in the fire. She cried over the children who blundered into the Time Wreck and died. It was she — you — who insisted that they fence it off. Don't you remember? Our teacher said you helped build it with your own hands, working until they bled. You gave people courage, she said. They were ashamed to do nothing when you worked so hard."

"That wasn't me," Mary said. "It was my great-great-grandma. I wish I was like her. I wish I could do the things she did. I wish I was as brave —"

"But you are her," they insisted. "You know you are. The old devil brought you back from the other side. He said so. We heard him. Why should he say so if it isn't true?"

"Because he's a liar," a voice said. Mary turned round and saw Kollos behind her. "Put on your hat. You don't want Prosson to see you. He's here, you know, looking for you. He has plans for you, the old devil."

"People keep telling me that," Mary complained, "but they won't say what exactly —"

"Because we don't know exactly: we can only guess. But knowing Prosson, I think you'll do well to keep out of his way, unless you want to be turned into a golden icon, a puppet carried aloft into a fight that doesn't concern you. Put on your hat."

"It's too big. It falls over my eyes."

Kollos plucked a hat from a nearby boy and put it on her head.

"There, that's better," he said, handing the old one to the boy, who protested angrily that it was too big for him too. Kollos shut him up, telling him he ought to be proud to help Mary Crumb.

"But you said she wasn't."

"No, I didn't. I said Prosson was a liar and so he is." Kollos looked around. His quick brown eyes noted the small crowd who had collected behind the children. Mary had pushed the new hat back from her forehead. Wisps of her orange hair, escaping from under the brim, burned gold in the bright sunlight. The men and women stared at her and then up at the statue.

Kollos raised his voice. "Prosson's telling everyone that Mary Crumb wants them to stay in Camptown. That she's come back to warn them that it's dangerous to go to the new settlement. Well, here she is. This is the girl who came over with him from the other side. Ask her. Ask her any questions you like. I don't know what she will say. I haven't coached her or threatened her in any way. I met her for the first time today, and the only words I have exchanged with her have been about a straw hat. She is free to say whatever she likes, to answer or to keep silent, as she wishes, without any hindrance from me."

His face was excited, intent. He looked like her mum when she was playing bingo. Gambling. "Speak clearly and slowly," he advised her, "or they won't understand you." He turned to the crowd and cried, "Silence! Silence for Mary Crumb! Let her speak."

Then he stepped away from her, leaving her alone. The people stared at her and waited.

23

Prosson, coming out of the Assembly Hall, paused on the top step and stared down at the people clustered around the statue. More and more people hurried over as he watched, and a noise like a swarm of bees rose into the air; a mixture of English and the old language.

It was impossible to hear what they said, impossible to tell what held their attention. Then a man's voice called out loudly, "Silence! Silence for Mary Crumb! Let her speak!"

What! Had they come to this so soon? Had his cunning rumors played so skillfully on their superstitions that they were expecting answers from the statue of a dead servant-girl?

Dark laughter welled up inside him. Fools, fools! They asked to be cheated.

"Friends, dear friends," he began softly. Too late. They did not even turn around. A child was

189

speaking, a child whose face he knew only too well, and all their attention was on her. She was standing at the foot of the statue, dressed in the simple, becoming dress of the workers. Her straw hat was pushed back to circle her head like a halo. Her high, clear voice like a bird's or an angel's, flew over the waiting crowds and reached his burning ears.

"I'm not Mary Coram come back. Honestly, I'm not. Don't believe anyone who tells you I am. It just isn't true. She's my great-great-grandma, and I'm proud of that. I hope there's something of her in me. But there's bits of my dad too, and bits of my mum, and everyone says I've got my uncle's nose. So I'm not just the mixture as before. I'm unique, that's what my teacher said. I'm me."

Somebody had stage-managed this, Prosson thought furiously, his eyes scanning the crowd for the face of an enemy.

Was Fate against him? He had followed her so long through the streets of her world, waited so patiently for a chance to bring her back here with him. He had almost given up hope, when she'd led him to a building site and he'd felt the familiar tingle and tilt of the world's edge. Then, just as he reached out to grab her, Calabal had pushed between them, and she'd slipped away into the splintering light and was lost.

He'd had his friends searching the woods for her the last three days until it was too dark to see their hands in front of their noses. He'd left men on every road into Camptown to catch her if she came that way, promising a good reward for her. At first light this morning, he had sent men to the ruins of the old town in case she was hiding there. No luck. He had begun to think she must have blundered into the Time Wreck and died there, like so many before her.

And here she was in front of him, undoing all his plans. For a moment his anger flared up murderously. He wanted to kill her, crush her, wipe her out of sunlight. Then he took a grip on himself. What to do? How to save the day?

A man was speaking now, a peasant farmer by the look of him, with a round, red simple face. "But Prosson says you fell into the Time Wreck and became unborn. Then, he says, you were born again on the other side. He warned us you might not remember the past. Everyone knows that the bad quakes scramble your brains. As for your uncle's nose — just look at your statue, Mary Crumb. Look at the paintings of you in the museum over there, and tell us then whose face you've got, nose and all."

"Well said, my man," Prosson called out and walked boldly through the crowd, which gave way for him. Mary saw him and her eyes widened. He hoped nobody would notice how she shrank from him.

"I've been looking for you everywhere, my dear child. I have been so worried about you," he said. His eyes were so kind and concerned that Mary thought she must have imagined the dark flames that had seemed to burn in them when he had first caught sight of her. "I was terrified that you'd fallen into the wreck and we'd lost you again. I searched the woods all afternoon, calling your name —"

"I didn't hear you," she lied. "I only heard you calling your dog."

He hid his anger. "I called you first, but when there was no answer, I called Calabal. I thought he might help me to find you. He's a good dog."

"Why did you hit him then?"

"Hit him? Me hit Calabal? I never would!" he protested, all injured innocence, conscious of the many eyes watching him.

"You did! I heard him squeal!"

"Oh that," he said easily. "That was the quake. Didn't you notice the ground shake and the electrical disturbance around the wreck? Perhaps you were still unconscious. Poor Calabal was frightened, most animals are. You always hear dogs howling after a quake."

There was a murmur of agreement from the crowd, a mention of cows jumping and pigs squealing and cats hiding under the bed.

It could be true, she thought.

"Poor Mary, your mind is confused," Prosson's hand was now on her arm, holding her gently with his strong fingers. "We've made a strange journey together, haven't we?" he said. He was glad to see her nod. He hoped the crowd had noticed it. The more he could link the two of them together in their minds, the better his chance of success. If only he could think more clearly, if only his head would stop aching. . . .

"A leap from one world to another, it's no wonder we feel disoriented." He went on, "What you need is rest. Sit here for a minute, my dear, here on the pedestal of your statue." He lifted her up onto the stone ledge by Mary Coram's feet. For a moment his face was close to hers. She felt his breath on her ear and thought she heard him whisper, "Do you want to see your home again? Only I can help you find your way back. Remember that." He straightened up and, raising his voice, went on, "Don't try to talk yet. You'll tire yourself. I will do the talking for you —"

"That would suit you, wouldn't it?" Kollos demanded, coming out of the crowd to stand before Prosson. "I'm afraid I must spoil your game, whatever it is. Mary has a voice of her own. She doesn't need you to interpret for her. She is here with my party. We are looking after her."

"I think not," Prosson said coldly. "I brought her over to our world. She is my responsibility, and I intend to take charge of her. Go away, Kollos, go back and tend your pigs, and take your rabble with you. We don't need you. I have friends here," he added pointedly, glancing at the crowd.

"And so have I," Kollos cried. "As many as you."

They glared at one another in the hot sunlight, two highly combustible men. Neither of them looked at Mary, sitting high up on the stone feet of the statue. She might have been a doll, she thought, for all the notice they took of her now.

She saw the crowd twitch like a dog disturbed by fleas as men wriggled their way through to the front, some for Prosson, some for Kollos. Mary saw the glint of metal in their hands, the hatred in their eyes.

"NO!" she shrieked, jumping to her feet and holding onto the statue to steady herself. "STOP IT, I TELL YOU!! STOP IT!"

To her surprise, the crowd fell silent. Somewhere a bird sang. Somewhere a child laughed and was hushed. They were all looking at her expectantly, and she couldn't think of anything to say.

"What sort of people are you?" she asked help-lessly. "You can't fight over who's going to look after me! That's stupid. Haven't you got a social worker or something?"

They stared at her in blank amazement. Even Prosson was silent, though she noticed his quick dark eyes looked everywhere, as if counting, add-ing up his friends and subtracting his enemies, doing battle sums in his head. He's mad, she thought.

"This is nothing to do with you, Mary Crumb," Kollos said, without taking his eyes off Prosson. "This is an old fight. Keep out of it."

"How can she, stuck up there in the middle of you?" a woman's voice called out. It was the old woman from the cart. "If you must fight, let's get the children away first. And the women, you'll need someone to bind up your wounds when it's over. And bury your dead."

She waddled forward. One of Prosson's sup-porters tried to stop her but she brushed him away as if he were a fly. Coming between Kollos and Prosson, she held her hands up to Mary.

"Come on, my chick! Come to Ma! I'll be your shoshell worker, whatever that may be. Jump, my pretty! I'll catch you, never fear."

Mary hesitated. Behind the old woman, other women had come forward and were plucking children out of the crowd. The older boys dodged away and had to be chased. The younger ones squirmed and kicked or lay on the ground, howling. The little girls squeaked and ran about like mice.

Prosson and Kollos, separated from their supporters by this living barrier of women and children, waited impatiently for them to get out of the way, their faces becoming more flushed and angry by the minute.

"Don't just stand there!" Prosson shouted, pushing at them with his hands. "Move! Move! Move!"

"Moo! Moo! Moo!" a boy mimicked, and people laughed. Mary saw Prosson's eyes burn in his heated face. He strode toward the offender and nearly tripped over an infant who'd been sitting unnoticed by his feet. With a roar of sheer rage, he picked the baby up in one hand and swung it over his head.

"PROSSON!" Mary screamed.

Her voice held him. Intending to dash the screaming infant onto the cobbles, he paused a moment, still holding the infant aloft and fending off anyone who tried to take it away, with a knife held in his free hand.

"Who called me?" he asked wildly. "Who was that?"

"Mary Coram," Mary said, looking into his mad eyes and trying not to show she was afraid. "Give the child to one of the women. If you do, I'll go with you, not with Kollos. I'll be on your side."

"You! You'll be on my side? And who are you?"

"You know me. You brought me over," she said, puzzled and afraid. "You were right about me. I — I am Mary Coram. Give the child to the woman, Prosson."

For some reason her words, meant to soothe, had the opposite effect.

"You impertinent squab!" he shouted. "Are you trying to manipulate *me*! You, the brat I found sniveling into the canal near your home. Do you think I don't know who you are? Do you think I didn't hear the boys singing — how did it go? 'Spooky Loonie, Mary Frewin, tell us what your ghosts are doing.' That was it — Frewin. Not Crumb, you can't even pronounce the name properly. You're no more Mary Crumb than my dog is. You're —"

He stopped in confusion, suddenly remembering that he had himself spread the rumor that she was Mary Crumb. It had been part of his great design, but he couldn't remember now what the plan was. His head ached so terribly. He was sick . . .

He stood there, swaying, staring at Mary without seeing her properly. The sunlight fell on her and on the statue behind her, changing them both to the same pale gold, seeming to make them one.

"Who is she?" he mumbled. "Who is Mary Crumb? Only a dead servant-girl, nothing more. Only a dead girl."

He did not notice that the sobbing infant had been taken away from him, and that the knife had dropped from his nerveless fingers. He was still staring at Mary when they led him away, his head turning over his shoulder until she was out of sight.

"I made her into a legend," he told the men who held him. "It was I who did it. They'd have forgotten her but for me. And what has she done in return? She has destroyed me. That is what she has done. Destroyed me."

24

"But where can he have gone?" Mary asked.

It was ten days since Prosson, looking back at her with his mad eyes, had been led away to the hospital. There he'd been put in a room on the first floor and given a sleeping pill to quiet his ravings, a nurse to sit by his bed, and a guard to sit outside his door.

"It must have been a long and tedious night," Belois had said. "Nobody blames them for wanting a hot drink. But to go off together —"

"They said he was deep asleep," Gally explained, excusing them, "and they locked the door before they went."

But they had forgotten the window and the apple tree outside. When they returned, they found the wind blowing into an empty room. Prosson had vanished.

"Forget him, Mary," everyone told her. "Be glad he's gone."

But she wasn't glad. She was furious with the nurse and the guard who had let him escape. She needed him if she was ever to get home. "Only I can help you find your way back," he'd said. Perhaps he had no intention of helping her. Perhaps, like her, he had been blinded by the fierce light and left with a spinning head and no memory of the way he'd come. But she had to ask him. The people here were kind, but this world was not her home. Her mother and father were not perfect, any more than she was. She knew people laughed at them, she often did herself. But they were hers, and she loved them.

"I want to go home," she said.

They sympathized but could not help her. None of them knew of a way across: most of them had given up searching for one long ago. It was too dangerous, they told her, looking worried. They'd made a great fuss of her, calling her a hero. "You saved the little boy's life," they said, and the boy's mother had hugged her, weeping with joy. "Stay with us, Mary Crumb. There'll always be a home for you here."

"I'm not Mary Crumb," Mary kept saying. "I only said I was because I thought it'd calm him down, see? My name's Mary Frewin, like Prosson said."

"Frewin or Crumb," they assured her, "it makes no difference. You'll always be welcome."

She couldn't help enjoying her popularity, the invitations and the gifts they kept pressing on her. Even Keet, whom she had thought stiff and unfriendly, had smiled at her warmly and said, "Don't stay here in Camptown. Come with us to the new settlement, Mary. We'll take good care of you. And your friends are coming."

Her friends? She thought of Nonny and Isobel back home, but of course he had meant her new friends, Gally and Belois. All week she had been helping them pack the things needed for the journey into large hampers and wooden boxes, while their parents, out at the farms, helped load up sacks of grain and potatoes onto the large wagons. Tomorrow Kollos would lead the wagons out on their journey to the new settlement. Just like a Western on television, Mary thought, and almost wished she was going with them. But she was not. It was all settled. She was going to stay with Dafre's sister and her husband in Wodol, a small village outside Camptown.

She sat on a large soft bundle tied with rope and watched Belois and Gally packing the last of the books into a cardboard box.

"Here, take this —" Belois said, handing Mary

one in a faded red cover. "Something to remember us by."

"She won't need anything to remember us by. She's coming with us," Gally insisted.

Mary shook her head. "You know I'm not. I'm staying with Lily and Hogan in Wodol. I told you."

"But you can't. You'd hate it there. Lily's kind but much older than Dafre, and Hogan is a fat oaf. I can't think why she married him. You'll soon be bored to tears. Come with us. All the best people are going. Me and Belois, for instance," Gally said, smiling at her. "Think how much you'll miss us when we've gone. There'll only be the dull people left, those who're afraid to get their feet wet. And the Drowlians, of course, who don't want to leave their farms. They're all right but very virtuous and strict —"

"Didn't you tell me that Prosson is a Drowlian?" Mary asked.

"Yes. His parents are farmers and very proud of him. They sent him to the best school in Camp-town — well, there are only two, but still, most Drowlians send their children to village schools. And was he grateful? This will show you the sort of person he was, even then. As soon as he got to college, he told everyone he was not really their son at all but a foundling, left on a doorstep in a basket —"

"Like Mary Coram!"

"As he was always pointing out. Kollos doesn't believe him. He thinks he just made it up to make himself more interesting, more romantic than a mere farmer's boy. But it could be true. Certainly he's nothing like any Drowlian I've ever met."

"Where is his parents' farm?" Mary asked. "Is it near here?"

"Why do you want to know?" Gally asked suspiciously. "You're not thinking of looking them up, I hope. Mary, leave it alone. The farm is in the middle of nowhere, right out in the country. Besides, they are very simple people and speak in the old language. I doubt if they have much English. Even if they know where Prosson is and agree to tell you, you won't be able to understand them. And they might try to keep you there."

"To keep me? You mean against my will?"

"Oh, I don't mean they'll actually tie you up or lock you in the attic, but they won't want you to go. Mary Crumb is an important part of their belief. That's Prosson's doing. He was a teacher once. That's when he wrote the books about Mary Crumb, three of them, each more fantastic than the last. I mean, I know she was a hero, but she was human. According to most accounts, she cried sometimes and lost her temper. He turned her into a blessed angel. He said she would come back one day in a blaze of light and bring prosperity and peace. And people believed him. A silly dreamy boy called Dummo said he'd seen her in your world, standing looking out. She waved at him, he said, and smiled."

"I'm afraid that was only me," Mary said apologetically. "I did wave at the ghosts sometimes, but they never waved back. I thought they couldn't see me."

Gally laughed. "Do you still think we're ghosts?"

She shook her head. "No. You're solid enough. How did Mary Coram die?"

"She caught a fever nursing the sick, according to most accounts. But Prosson claims there was an old book in the museum library, giving a full description of her falling into the wreck and vanishing. He says he came across it when he was a student. There's no way to prove it, one way or another. The book is now lost. Or so he says."

"You think he made it up? Why should he?"

"Oh, I don't know. To make a name for himself, I suppose," Gally said. "Father told me Prosson always wanted to be a leader of men, even at college, but nobody would follow him. He said he lacked the necessary charm, being cold and sharp and commonplace, like a kitchen knife. People didn't trust him. They were afraid he'd cut their fingers. That was when he became obsessed with Mary Crumb, who'd had the charm he lacked, a charm that reached out across the grave. Father says he used to stand and stare at her statue and watch the country women on market days touch its feet for luck. Once he saw him touch the statue himself, as if hoping the charm would rub off on him. And a little of it did. Father says people laughed at him behind his back for loving a dead girl, but they liked him better for his obsession. It made him more human."

Belois shook her head. "I don't think so. I think he was already planning how to use the super-stitions that clung to her to gain power and glory for himself. That's when he started writing the books about her, to link his name with hers. Like that one —"

"Is this one of his?" Mary opened the one Belois had given her. "I can't read it," she said. "The letters are all funny."

"It's in the old language," Belois told her. "I can't find the one in English, but I thought you might like to take this home with you to show people."

"What does it say?"

Belois shrugged. "I only know a few words of

Drowlian. I read the last one in English. It was wild, like a mad poem without rhymes. Splinters of light slicing up the dark, and a bright angel descending from the sky with her hair on fire — that could mean you, Mary Crumb, with your red hair. Or a silver flying-ship with a burning tail. Who can tell? I think he was already half mad by then. This is the first one, so it is probably more sensible. Perhaps someone will translate it for you."

Mary thanked her and put the book carefully in her backpack.

"She won't need his stupid book. She's coming with us!" Gally cried. "You must, Mary. It's going to be such fun. We're all going to follow Kollos, hundreds of us. You and Belois can ride in the carts. Every night, we'll sit around the campfire and sing the old songs and tell stories. And you can teach us new ones. Please come!"

For a moment, she was tempted and nearly said yes. But when he said softly, smiling into her eyes, "I'll miss you so much, Mary Crumb," she was suddenly embarrassed. She thought of Edward Potts who had smiled just so at Miss Timpson.

He doesn't mean it, she thought.

Yesterday she'd asked Gally to write something

in her autograph book. He'd taken the book from her curiously and asked her what it was for.

"People write in it. Poems and things like that. You could put that poem you recited to me in the garden, the one you had to learn at school."

"Which one was that?" he'd asked. "We had to learn so many."

He had forgotten. She remembered it so clearly; the smiling face of the boy lying on his back in the long grass, gazing up at her with shining eyes; the summer leaves all around them, casting green shadows on his warm face. The words of the poem: "Your brightness blinds me, Mary Crumb, to the colder charms of the girls at home. . . ."

"Oh, it doesn't matter," she'd said quickly, hiding her disappointment. "Write anything."

So having read and laughed over the poems already in the book, he'd written this for her:

"Roses are red.

So are ghosts' ears,

Don't tease poor Mary

Or she'll burst into tears —"

A poem for a child. Oh well, she thought. Mum's always saying I'm too young for boyfriends. Perhaps she's right. But I'm older than I was.

Old enough to know that Gally would not miss her for long in all the excitement of the great journey. After all, he'd forgotten her that day in the marketplace, when she could have done with his support. "Where were you?" she'd asked him later and he told her he'd gone off to visit his old friends. Girlfriends, probably. No, he wouldn't miss her for long.

But there were people at home who would miss her, people who had known her forever and wouldn't have forgotten her. Mum and Dad, for sure. Nonny and Isobel and her other friends at school. Even Miss Timpson might be missing her a little. "I want to go home," she said.

Early next morning, before the sun was out of the trees, she stood waving goodbye as the procession set off along the dusty road. There was Kollos on a fine gray horse at their head, followed by Keet driving a wagon with Dafre sitting beside him, holding a small boy on her lap. More wagons, rattling and jingling as they jolted over the ruts. Even Ma was going, driving a small cart piled with sacks and bundles and a crate with two chickens in it. Then came the cattle, followed by whooping men on horseback, kicking up the dust in the watchers' faces. When it cleared, Mary saw Gally, sitting astride a dancing pony, smiling down at her.

"Come with us, Mary Crumb!" he shouted.

She laughed and shook her head and stood watching while he rode on. He looked back three times over his shoulder. Then one of the men called to him, and he galloped off into a cloud of dust.

25

It was only a month since the wagons left, but it seemed longer. Gally was right. Dafre's sister Lily was kind but dull. Her husband Hogan was a silent man, opening his mouth only to put food in it or to yawn.

"He works hard," Lily said. "There's a lot of work to do in the woods, felling trees, clearing the undergrowth. It's no wonder he's ready for bed after his supper."

They lived in a village five miles from Camptown, a small untidy cluster of wooden bungalows. No shops. No cinema. No television. Not even a café. Nothing to do, except climb the trees.

There were plenty of those. That was why Mary had chosen to accept this offer of a home, rather than one in Camptown, where at least there was a market and a dance hall and a river to swim in.

Somewhere, on the other side of the wood, was the field with the Time Wreck.

"I don't mind you going to the playground," Lily told her. "That's where all our children go in the holidays. There are swings and seesaws and ropes to climb. And a hut where you can shelter when it rains. But don't go any further. It's not safe. We don't want to lose you."

The playground was in a clearing on the edge of the woods. Every day when it was fine, Mary went there with the other children. They were a mixed lot of Crumbs, Drowlians, and Neptals. She did not join in their games. She did not have her lunch with them but climbed up a tree to eat her sandwiches by herself. No doubt they thought she was standoffish. Certainly the old woman in charge of the playground disapproved of her, but being a Drowlian with little if any English, could only shake her head at Mary and mumble under her breath. Mary smiled and spread her hands and went on climbing her tree.

As she sat high up on a branch, completely hidden except for a dangling leg, she watched them through the leaves. At first, they glanced up from time to time, as if to check she was still there, but after a few days, they no longer bothered. The old woman went on with her knitting.

211

The children played and squabbled and forgot about the unfriendly stranger in the chestnut tree. Then Mary climbed down and slipped off through the trees to explore the woods. She didn't think they missed her. She was always back in time, and they never said anything.

She didn't go far at first: she was frightened of getting lost. She dropped tiny scraps of paper to mark the way she went, but often could not find them again. One day, as she stood hopelessly trying to decide which of three paths to take, she heard a noise behind her. Turning around, she saw a boy dodge out of sight.

"I saw you, Jippy!" she called. "It's no good hiding."

He came out from behind a tree, a thin young Neptal boy, about eight years old, with silky black hair and a pale brown skin. He limped as he came toward her. She remembered being told that the branch of a tree had fallen on his foot once and the bones had not set properly. It did not seem to hurt him when he walked, but he avoided playing rough games with the other boys, and was often on his own.

"What are you doing here?" she asked.

"Just walking."

"You were following me, weren't you? Spying on me? Why, Jippy? Did somebody tell you to?"

"No. I wasn't spying! I wasn't!" he said earnestly. "It was just — just something to do."

She smiled, understanding immediately. "I used to do that when my friends were too busy for me. I'd follow people all over Islington, pretending to be a detective or an escaped prisoner creeping through enemy country. Who were you pretending to be?"

"A skyman, crashed into a strange world, seeing his first native."

"That's me, I suppose?" she asked.

"Yes. He wouldn't know if he could trust you, you see, that's why he was hiding."

"Oh, he can trust me," she said lightly.

"Would you like to see his wreck?" he asked. "I can take you there."

After about twenty minutes, the woods thinned out and Mary could smell again the acrid stink of the wreck. Jippy led her through a hole in the high fence, and there it was, huge and motionless and black, against the blue sky.

"I often come here," Jippy told her. "I like to sit and watch the false fire on the wreck when there's a quake. Nobody else comes here. They're frightened."

"It's sensible to be frightened of something

213

dangerous," Mary said reprovingly. "You shouldn't come here, Jippy."

"It's dangerous for you too," he said, laughing at her. "But you were trying to find it, weren't you, Mary Crumb?"

"I thought Prosson might come here," she admitted. "I don't know where else to look."

"Prosson!" Now Jippy was frightened, looking around as if he expected Prosson to rise smoking out of the ground. "Dad said he'd gone off to the hills to join the other outcasts. He won't come here, will he? They say he kills boys. They say he throws them into the wreck and you can hear their bones rattle all the way down to hell. Let's get back among the trees so we can hide." He seemed to feel he had to explain his sudden lack of courage and added, "I can't run very fast, you see."

"I'm glad to see you've got some sense," she said, smiling and taking his hand. "Come on, let's get back. And you must promise me you won't come here again, Jippy, do you hear?"

"What about you?"

"Prosson won't hurt me," she said, wishing she could be certain of this. "Besides, your dad may be right. Where are those hills he talked about? Are they near here?"

He shook his head and told her they were on the other side of Camptown. "A hundred miles away, or fifty, something like that," he said vaguely. "I've never seen them."

Mary sighed. No train, no bus, and she could not ride a horse, even if she borrowed one. Besides, she had a feeling he would come back to the wreck, just as she had. It was the gateway between the two worlds.

As they walked back, Jippy kept warning her that she mustn't trust Prosson. However, he promised not to tell anyone where she'd gone.

"I don't tell tales," he said, but he looked worried. The first day he followed her. She could hear the bushes rustling behind her, but this time, when she looked around she saw nothing but trees and leaves.

"Jippy, I know it's you!" she called.

No answer.

"Jippy, don't be mean. You're frightening me."

"It's only sensible to be frightened of something dangerous," he said smugly, stepping out of some bushes.

"Oh, go away," she said, laughing, but he came with her until they could see glimpses of the field through the trees when he told her he'd wait for her there.

"But Jippy, I'm trying to get back to my own world. If there's a chance, I'll have to go at once. I won't be able to let you know. Go home, there's a good boy."

"How will I be able to tell if you're safe home or dead in the wreck?" he asked dismally, and she could not think of an answer.

"I'll be all right," she said.

She went every morning to the field above the wreck and waited for Prosson. Sometimes she had a feeling that Jippy still followed her through the woods, but she never caught him again.

The days were hot and still, the wreck motionless under a blue sky. No false fire flickered over its twisted girders. The strips of reflecting material hardly stirred in the windless air. It looked harmless from a distance, but when she came close, she began to feel nervous. There was something monstrous about the wreck rearing up above her. Her skin began to feel odd, tight and tingling, and the ground shifted slightly under her feet.

She retreated to the higher ground and sat down, looking at the wreck, studying it carefully. It was not possible to see inside it. She could not tell whether it was hollow, with all its innards burned out, or whether it was possible, having climbed up one side, to walk across to the other. Not that there was anything on the other side worth the trouble. Several times, she had walked all around the wreck, a long and difficult walk over the rough and creviced ground.

In places, creepers grew halfway up the sides; in others the oily loops of black plastic drooped down toward the earth. The girders, she saw, were made of a flat, pierced metal, about fourteen centimeters wide. Wide enough to walk on if you had a head for heights. Most of them were twisted and many broken, and some of the uprights leaned sideways, as if considering falling down. Everywhere, the sky showed through them, a flat, clear blue.

No. Not quite everywhere.

At first, she thought it was a cloud she saw between two girders at the far side of the wreck, a low, luminous cloud shining like mist in the sun, an oddly bright cloud that dazzled her eyes so that she could no longer see clearly.

The sun still shone above her head, the sky was still blue everywhere else. Funny.

She walked around to the back, but could see

nothing to account for it. No cloud. No mist. Nobody standing on the girder and shining a strong light through sheets of gauze. After all, why should they? She must have imagined it. Yet when she walked back to where she'd been sitting before, she could still see it. It was always there. She had only to sit on the boulder and look across to the girders on the far side of the wreck. There, between two uprights and a loop of black plastic, she would see it shining, whatever it was — a reflection of the sun, perhaps, an optical illusion, or the gateway between two worlds, elusive and unobtainable.

On the tenth day, Prosson came. It was a hot day. Mary was sitting on the grass, leaning against the boulder, when she heard a rustling of paper beside her and, looking around, saw Calabal with his nose in her backpack, trying to tear the paper off her sandwiches.

"Hey!" she cried, and a deeper voice joined in, speaking in the old language.

"Vod! Vod ak, Calabal! Bahla ruff!"

The dog sprang away, his tail between his legs, his lips curling back from his teeth in a snarl. Looking up, Mary saw Prosson, tall and dark against the bright sky. Before she could move, he sat heavily down in the grass beside her. His hand touched her arm and he moved it down to circle her wrist with his thumb and forefinger, like a bracelet ready to snap shut.

"I hear you have been looking for me, Mary Frewin," he said.

26

Prosson looked terrible. His eyes were bloodshot. His skin, seen so close, was badly creased, as if he'd tossed and turned all night until not only his sheets but his very skin was rumpled.

She tried to speak, but all that came out of her mouth was the squeak of a frightened mouse.

"Are you laughing at me?" he demanded, his eyes blazing with such anger that she cowered away from him, trying to free her hand. "Are you?" he said again, shaking her.

"No."

"It sounded like it."

"It was a hiccup."

"Oh," he said, and seemed to lose interest. His grip on her wrist relaxed, and he sat staring down at the grass without saying anything. Calabal, safely out of reach, lay down, rested his nose on his paws and sighed, as if prepared for a long wait.

Mary was silent. It did not seem the right time to ask a favor.

Prosson was talking again, his voice now so low that she had to strain to hear what he said. "A lost chance, a missed boat, gone forever."

"What has?"

"Everything I dreamed of. We could have ruled this world together, you and I, Mary Crumb. I had great plans. . . ."

"What plans?" she asked curiously.

At first she thought he had not heard her. With his free hand, he fumbled at his head, as if trying to find something in his hair, an escaped idea, perhaps or a memory.

"A party," he said at last.

"A party?" she exclaimed, surprised.

"A political party, you silly child, not one with balloons! With you by my side, a figurehead, an inspiration, people would have flocked like sheep . . . sheep to the slaughter — no, that's wrong. What was I going to say? I forget. I forget everything." He glared across at the wreck. "I have been in that pot too often. My brains are scrambled. Why did I come here, Mary Crumb? Was it to see you?"

"You promised you'd show me how to get home," she told him.

"Is that why you waited for me? I thought you

would go with the others to the new settlement. A long and difficult journey, it's true. But you'll find the journey home more difficult, though shorter. One false step may end it all in a moment —"

"But you said you knew the way."

"You've done the journey yourself. Why do you need me?"

"I fell over. I must've knocked myself out because the next thing I knew I was here on the grass."

"Poor Mary Crumb. Or should I say Mary Frewin?" He leaned forward, "Which are you? Tell me. . . . No, it doesn't matter. Mary, Mary, you have ruined me."

"But I didn't do nothing!"

"You're only a child. I bear you no grudge. Come on, let's get you home to bed." He picked up her backpack. "Is this your bag? Put it on, put it on. That's right. Now come on! We must hurry."

Still holding her by the wrist, he jerked her to her feet and ran, pulling her behind him and shrieking, "Mind the cracks! Mind the cracks!"

He's mad, she thought, stumbling through the long grass, unable to free her hand.

"Please stop!" she cried breathlessly. "I can't come — not right now. I haven't told — anyone. I haven't said — goodbye!"

The wreck reared up above them now, like a

broken mechanical beast, with a harsh stink that caught in her throat and made her eyes water. Prosson lifted her up as easily as if she were a doll and sat her on the girder above his head. She heard the dog barking. A moment later there was a scrabble of paws beside her, and there was Calabal, crouching on the narrow beam and snarling down at his master.

"Lift him down! It's not safe! He'll fall!"

"Not he," Prosson said, and looking into the dog's eyes, added something in the old language. Then he pulled himself up on the other side of Mary and got shakily to his feet. Holding out his arms on either side, he began dancing away from her, singing, "One false step! One false step! That's the way to go!" in a high cracked voice.

She watched him in amazement, expecting him to overbalance at any moment but he reached the nearest upright safely, and holding onto it, swung around to face her.

I've missed my chance, she thought. I should've jumped down onto the grass and run for the woods the moment he turned his back.

As if reading her mind, he said, "Don't try and run away. I ordered Calabal to guard you just now. He won't let you move unless I say so. I trained him well."

Mary scowled at the dog, who was watching her

with hot brown eyes, "I thought you were my friend, you ungrateful dog. You'll not get a crumb out of me again," she muttered.

Prosson laughed. "A Crumb — no, we won't make a Crumb out of you, Mary. Still, I like you. You don't snivel and whine." He paused for a moment, looking down at her, then said briskly, "Hold onto that vertical pole behind you and stand up. That's right. Now turn around carefully and look at the wreck. If you feel giddy, shut your eyes for a moment, and then try again. Go on doing this until you no longer feel giddy."

She turned and looked.

It was like nothing she had imagined. Whatever this had once been, it was now only a damaged hollow shell, half buried in the earth. Above her head, shreds of some glittering substance clung to it, as if festive decorations had been torn away in a hurry. Stalactites of melted plastic hung down above narrow platforms, while in dark corners, blackened wires clustered like nests of snakes with their heads pulled off. Far below her feet, small trees, their branches pale as roots, struggled out of a dark and shifting stew to reach the light above.

Somewhere, somebody screamed.

"Who was that?" Prosson asked sharply.

"It wasn't me, was it?" Mary asked, trembling and confused.

"Of course it wasn't. It came from the woods."

"Perhaps it was an owl."

"All the owls are asleep now," he told her irritably. "Come on, we must hurry. There's a quake coming soon. Can't you feel it in the air? Now listen: follow me exactly. Put your feet where I put mine. Bend down when I bend down. Stop when I stop. Don't try to think for yourself; what looks like an easier way may lead to your death. There's danger all around us, in all dimensions. Remember that."

He turned and began walking slowly along the girder away from her. She was so frightened that she could not move. Her fingers clutched the upright so tightly that she felt she would never be able to uncurl them again. Something cold and wet touched her free hand, and she cried out.

"Was that you, that noise?" Prosson demanded, without turning.

"Sorry. Calabal touched my hand with his nose and startled me."

"Where are you? You're supposed to be close behind me." Prosson walked forward until he could hold the next upright and looked back at her. "You haven't moved!" he said in disgust. "What's the matter? Are you frightened?"

"No," she lied. "But supposing Calabal tries to pass me and pushes me over?"

"Hold tight to that pole, and I'll call him to me," he said.

"I am holding tight."

Prosson whistled to the dog, and Calabal, squirming past Mary, walked carefully to his master. Prosson grabbed hold of his collar and pulled him past him. "Now he can lead the way," he said. "He knows it better than I do. Come on. I'm not waiting for you."

With that he turned and followed the dog along the next girder. Mary, forcing her fingers to let go of the pole, began walking after them, trying not to look down, terrified of falling. At first she crept forward like a snail, but then, finding that she did not feel giddy even when she looked right down to the pale trees below her, she gained confidence. Walking more quickly, she soon caught up with them.

The dog led them, his claws clicking against the hard girders or padding softly over small moss-covered platforms. Once he lowered himself onto his belly and crept forward, his head down, his tail straight. Then Prosson also flattened himself onto the girder and began wriggling forward like a snake.

"Copy me!" he called.

So she did. The rough surface caught at her shirt

and grazed her chin. Ahead of her, she saw Prosson's feet in their worn leather sandals pushing him forward a little at a time. So much effort for so little gained. No wonder he was panting. She began to pity snakes and all creatures who had to crawl on their bellies. But, of course, snakes were quick. Snakes could rear up like floor lamps and balance on their tails. . . . What would happen if she sat up now? Supposing none of it were true and they were just having her on?

"We can get up now," Prosson said. "Step onto that platform. Be careful —"

His warning came too late. Mary, glad to be released from their crawl, had got to her feet too quickly. She staggered. Her left leg slipped down between the girder and the platform.

It hurt! Oh, how it hurt!

Somebody was shouting something, but pain confused her. She felt as if a swarm of wasps were attacking her foot. Then Prosson grabbed her under the arms and pulled her safely into the middle of the platform. The pain in her foot lessened, became no more than a prickle. She glanced down at it — and screamed.

Attached to her leg was the foot of a crone, a shriveled sack of knobbly bones and wormlike veins, with horny toenails like claws. . . .

Before her scream died away in the quiet air, the

foot started changing again. The yellowy color grew pink and fresh, the skin smooth if somewhat dirty, the flesh beneath firm and young again. She wriggled the toes, turned the foot one way and another and compared it with her right foot. It matched. "My sandal's gone," she said.

Prosson exploded. "Is that all you can say?" he demanded. "You nearly lost your foot for good. If it hadn't been for me, if I hadn't snatched you up in time, it would have been too late for your foot to change back again. There'd just be bones and gristle at the end of that leg. That's all. Just bones and gristle."

"Oh. Oh, thank you," she whispered, and began to shake.

"It's all right," he said gently. "It's all right, Mary Crumb."

"Did I step into the future?" she asked. "Will my foot really look so horrible when I'm old?"

"Not if you take care of it," he said, laughing, "and keep your toenails cut."

"Do yours —" she began, and stopped, biting her lip.

"No. My feet do not look like that. I hope they never will. That foot looked at least a hundred years old and badly neglected." He glanced up at the sky and frowned. "There's a storm coming, or a quake. I'm sorry, Mary. No time to rest. We must go on."

Then it happened. He stepped away from her, tripped over Calabal who was lying behind him, and tumbled off the other side of the platform. Calabal sprang to his feet, leaped onto a nearby girder, and raced away.

"Prosson!" Mary shouted. "Prosson!"

She scrambled across and hung over the edge. She saw with relief that he had caught hold of a strut supporting the platform and had drawn his legs up towards his chest. Lying flat on her stomach, she reached down her hand.

He looked at it and shook his head.

"I'm too heavy for you," he said.

"I'm strong. I'm stronger than I look."

He shook his head again. "I'd only pull you down with me. I never wanted to hurt you, Mary Crumb. Never."

Still keeping his feet curled up beneath him, he began to swing himself backward and forward on the strut as if on a trapeze.

"What are you doing?" she asked, trembling.

"Trying — to avoid — the future," he called back. "It's below us — where you — put your foot. I don't — want to die — not yet. If I can — miss it — and find the past —" he twisted his head toward her

229

and gave a crooked smile, "I'll — see you in—a hundred years, Mary Crumb! Look out for me!"

He let go and flew in wide arc, falling, falling, and dwindling as he fell . . . a boy, a child, a baby falling out of the too-big clothes to rest naked in a nest of leaves, then tumbling out of sight. . . . Down must come baby, cradle and all.

27

Mary crouched on the platform and cried. She cried because she was terrified. She also cried for Prosson. He'd been a wicked man, everyone had told her so. He'd driven young Crumbs to their deaths in his pursuit of a mad dream. He cared for nothing except power — power and Mary Crumb.

Still, he had saved her, Mary Frewin, when she had slipped. It was thanks to him she still had two feet. "I never wanted to hurt you," he'd said at the end. She wondered which Mary he'd thought he was talking to.

At least he had managed to swing himself into the past. Better to be an unborn baby than a pile of bones. Bad and mad he might be, but she couldn't help feeling sorry for him. Sorry for herself too. Perched on a narrow platform, surrounded by forces she didn't understand, terrified to move a finger in case it turned to bone or shrank back through childhood until it vanished. . . . Like Prosson had vanished. . . .

No. She mustn't panic. She must think.

She shut her swollen, aching eyes, but it did not help. She could find no ideas inside her head, only scraps of thoughts and words, Prosson's words: "There's a quake coming, can't you feel it in the air?. . . . I'm not waiting for you!"

He hadn't waited, she thought, and saw again Prosson's body tumbling, dwindling, caught for a moment in a cradle of leaves, then gone in a rush of green —

A rush — the word echoed in her mind. "Don't rush at things," her mother was always telling her. "Look before you leap. Test the water with your fingers before you jump into the bath —"

Test it, she thought, looking down at her hands. One finger would do, no need to be extravagant. One finger or, better still, a pencil? Carefully she unstrapped her backpack and looked inside. A pencil, a pen, her autograph book.

If she tore a page into strips and wrote something at one end, she could use it like litmus paper to test the time around her. If the paper crumbled and the writing faded with age, then so would she.

If the paper vanished completely, it would mean it hadn't yet been made in the past. . . . Or would it? It might've been burnt up and blown away at some time in the future.

Her head was beginning to ache. Had to go on. Couldn't stay here forever.

Now if the *writing* vanished, it would mean it hadn't yet been written. That was better. She could use a page from her autograph book. She took it out of her backpack.

Gally's silly verse — no, she didn't want to risk losing that. Nor Nonny's self-portrait entitled Your Friend Forever. . . . Nor Isobel's 2 Y's U R, 2 Y's U B, I C U R, 2 Y's 4 me, which she thought was very clever, even if Nonny said it must be in every autograph book in the world.

She turned the pages slowly, reading and remembering, wanting to cry in case she never saw her old friends again. Stupid. She knew she was wasting time. She knew she was waiting for something, someone to save her. But there was nobody here but her.

She ripped out the page on which was written "with all the best wishes, Freda Timpson," folded it carefully lengthwise, and tore it again into three narrow strips. She held one of the strips up in the air as far as she could reach. It fluttered gently in the wind, but the writing was still there. The ink had not faded. The paper had not yellowed.

233

Safe to stand up? How long did it take ink to fade and paper to yellow? Ten years? Fifty years? Have to risk it.

She rose carefully to her feet. Nothing happened. The hair she plucked from her head was orange, not gray or white. Encouraged, she looked around, wondering which way to try first. There was a choice of three girders, but none of them seemed to lead anywhere in particular. A slight mist had risen. It was no longer easy to see right across the wreck.

She chose at random and crept forward like a snail, using the strips of paper like antennae to test any space before she moved into it. Once the writing seemed to fade away and she stopped in terror. But it was only a veil of mist: when the wind blew it away again, she could read quite clearly Miss Timpson's best wishes.

She tested above her head, in front of her, and to either side, but forgot her feet. When they started to ache and tingle, she thought it was because she was tired. Suddenly she started to sway and stumble. Glancing down, she saw with horror that she was toddling and toppling on shrinking feet, feet rapidly becoming as tiny and tender and pink as a baby's —

She screamed and flung herself forward onto an upright, clutching it with her hands and knees and forcing herself upward until her feet were themselves again. She saw the strips of paper she had dropped fluttering in the wind, down and down until they suddenly vanished.

A dog barked.

Looking up, she saw Calabal gazing down at her from a small platform above her head. He looked the same as always, shaggy and humpbacked, no older, no younger. How had he survived? How had *he* known which girder to choose, which to avoid? Perhaps some canine instinct warned him of danger, some shiver in the air, some minute alteration in the stink of the wreck. Or perhaps he merely remembered the way he had been before.

"Calabal! Help me! Wait for me!" she called, but he jumped off the platform onto an adjoining girder and padded away.

Painfully, scraping her hands and feet, she pulled herself up onto the platform and sat for a moment, panting and whimpering. She could see the dog still moving away from her on the girder, his tail between his legs.

"Calabal!"

He stopped and looked back at her.

"Wait for me!"

He did not want to wait. He barked at her, sharp, nervous barks, then put his head back and howled like a wolf. The wild cry went through her head like a cold wind, waking old nightmares from their sleep. He was staring past her now, the fur on his shoulders standing up in a thick ruff. Turning, she saw blue fire flickering toward her on the girders and heard the sparks sing. Prosson had been right; there was a quake coming, coming fast. She leapt to her feet in a panic and ran toward Calabal, shouting at him to hurry.

He did not need a second telling but turned and raced away. Once he stopped and looked back at her. Then he leaped down onto a lower girder running at right angles to the one they were on and set off again at high speed. Mary followed. The flames were all around her now, on the girders above and below. She could feel them tickling her heels, but she had no breath left for screaming.

A sudden flash of lightning dazzled her, and she was falling, falling into darkness. The blue flames disappeared. She could only see the wreck dimly now, like a shadowy scaffolding whirling past. She snatched at one of the girders, but her fingers slipped. A fiery red moon shot up into the sky and hung there, like a flower on a stalk.

She landed on something soft that gave way beneath her with a harsh ripping noise. This was followed by a loud pattering and a smell of dust. Then silence, except for a soft rushing sound like waves stirring the pebbles on a beach. The sky above her head was gray, and the red moon now shone low in the sky on her left. The thing on which she was lying rocked gently beneath her. It was made of some sort of material, a fine net from the feel of it, and was badly torn at one side so that it hung askew. Every time she moved, it kept tearing and sagging, until finally it deposited her quite gently onto the ground.

As she sat there, trying to collect her wits, she heard a dog bark.

"Calabal?" she called. "Calabal, is that you?"

She thought she heard a movement but could see nothing. She seemed to be enclosed in some gloomy tunnel or tent, full of thin gray hangings that obscured her sight and gave off clouds of dust when she touched them. She heard something move again, quite near, and was suddenly afraid.

Then the hangings shook and parted in front of her, and she saw the huge shadow of a man.

"What the devil's happened here?" he demanded. "What have you done?"

"Nothing!" she cried, backing away.

"How did all this come down? Are you hurt? Are there any more of you up there?" he asked, pushing the netting away so that he could look up. A cloud of dust obliterated him and set him coughing. Mary ducked under the hangings and crept past him unnoticed.

She was in a sort of tunnel or narrow passage. She could see light at the end and started to run. The rushing sound was louder now, and she heard the dog bark again. Then she was out in the open and running down the pavement of a street, a proper street, with tall buildings on either side and cars parked. The streetlights above her head glowed like flowers against the dark sky. A café opposite the building site had lights in its windows, and people inside, laughing and talking. . . . It had been daylight when she had seen it last, the scaffolding, the tunnel over the pavement, the café opposite.

Better go. She could hear the man coming.

She fled down the pavement, with Calabal running beside her, barking excitedly and wagging his tail. When they were around the corner, she slowed down, took him by the collar, and they walked on together, turned another corner, crossed another road. When they were walking beside iron railings that looked familiar, she stopped. No sign of the large man. They had left him behind. There should be a notice —

Yes, here it was — CORAM'S FIELDS.

She knelt down and hugged Calabal, resting her cheek on his dusty head. "We're back, Calabal! Back in London!" she cried joyfully. "Just a little walk and we'll be home again —" Although, of course it wasn't his home, poor dog.

"Never mind," she said, comforting him. "I'll manage something, somehow."

They started walking back together, the dirty girl in her odd clothes and the wolflike dog. They did not notice the curious looks people gave them as they passed. They did not know what was waiting for them at Cloudsley Towers.

28

The pavement was hard and cold beneath her bare feet, but she walked jauntily, her hand resting lightly on Calabal's collar. She was going home. It did not matter that her eyes played tricks, that at times the neat Islington streets filled with rubble, broken towers reared up against the sky, and she saw once again the dusty ruined town of Izel.

Hallucinations were only to be expected after a quake, Gally had told her, when she'd said that she'd kept seeing things in Izel that reminded her of Islington; the shape of a roof, a misspelled shop sign, even the faces of her old friends echoed in the new.

"You'll find your eyes are haunted by distorted visual memories," he told her. "You'll see things that are somewhere else, in some other time, perhaps in a dream. Mad things. Silly things. Nothing to worry about. It will pass in a day or two."

So she walked on, ignoring the cracks, looking calmly at a red-headed boy she passed, who might have been Gally, except that his eyes glanced at her coldly, which Gally's had never done.

How long would she go on seeing him in other boys' faces? How long would it be before another boy recited poetry in her praise? Dear Gally, let him build his log hut in the new settlement and find some girl to cook his meals and wash his socks and plant potatoes in the mud. It wasn't what she wanted, but she wished him well.

This was what she wanted, this bustling city, the windows lit up in the buildings around her, the people talking in the familiar London voices, and the red buses trundling by. Home.

She could see the top of Cloudsley Towers rising up behind the houses, and suddenly she was nervous. This was the street she walked down every day on her way back from school, and yet she felt like a stranger. People coming out of the pub brushed past her as if they did not know she was there. A staggering man stepped heavily on her foot and did not apologize when she yelped with pain. She began to feel she was invisible.

Now a man and a woman came out of the Red Dragon Café, glanced at her indifferently, and walked away down the pavement, hand in hand. Who were they? Why did she feel she knew them well? As they passed under the streetlight, she recognized Freda Timpson and Edward Potts.

"Miss! Sir!" she cried. "It's me!"

Calabal raced past her, barking excitedly. Edward, seeing the dog's teeth, thrust Freda behind him, shouted, "No!" and raised a hand holding something —

"Don't!" Mary shrieked, running up. She grabbed the dog by his collar and pulled him behind her, much as Edward had pushed Freda Timpson, both of them protecting the thing they loved. "He saved my life. He's a good dog. Don't hurt him!"

Edward said, blinking at her through his spectacles, "It's only a folded newspaper. Look!" He held it out to show her.

"Let me see," she said, taking it out of his hand.

"Hey!" Edward protested. "I haven't read that yet. I wasn't going to hurt your dog. I like dogs."

"It's Mary! Edward, it's Mary!" Freda Timpson cried, stepping out from behind him.

"So it is," Edward said, staring. "I didn't recognize her. She's covered with dust, look at her hair! What is it, Mary? Has there been an accident? Are you hurt?"

"I don't think so . . . I feel a bit funny. It's only the hallucinations, I expect. Gally warned me. You were right, Mr. Potts." Her words came tumbling out. Her eyes were as bright as if she had a fever. "You were right about the other world. That's where I've been all this time. Well, I expect you know that. Nonny and Isobel must've told everyone. They were there. They must've seen me vanish, just like Mary Crumb. Was it in all the papers? I don't suppose there's anything after all this time. . . ."

Not noticing the glances they exchanged, she looked down at the paper in her hand, tilting it sideways to catch the light.

"Come with us, Mary," Miss Timpson said gently. "Edward's car is parked just down the road. We'll take you home, my dear. You're not well —"

"This is an old paper! Isn't it? *Isn't* it?" Mary cried. Her hand began shaking.

"It's today's," Edward told her. "See — The Evening Standard. Friday, 22nd September. Come, let's get you home. It's late. Your parents must be worried."

"It can't be!" Mary muttered furiously. "*It's not true!* You're joking, aren't you?" Her hand was shaking so much she could not read the print.

"Here, let me hold it for you," Freda Timpson

said, steadying the paper with her hand, so that for a moment Mary saw it clearly.

Friday, 22nd September 1995.

She stood staring at it, remembering the words she had written in her diary on that night — "Friday, 22nd September. Tomorrow I am going to Coram's Fields to try and find my great-great-grandma's new world. If I never come back, I hope Isobel is sorry that she refused to come and watch me vanish so she could tell Mum and Dad and get some money from the newspapers for her story."

Isobel had changed her mind the next morning. She and Nonny had come with her. Isobel and Nonny and the Bad-Dog Boys had followed them all the way to Coram's Fields. And then — she could remember it all so clearly, the cracked field and the wreck, and the weeks that had followed. Now that time had gone, burned up by the small blue flames of a quake. And here she was, arrived back from her adventures on the day before she had started out, with nothing to show for it.

"It's not fair!" she shouted.

Freda and Edward exchanged glances again, and this time she noticed. She had seen that sort of glance before, the Poor Mary glance people used to exchange whenever she'd talked about her ghosts. Poor Mary, that's what they were thinking. Poor mad girl.

"Let's take you home," Freda said. "It's late and you look tired —"

"We're nearly there. That's my car, the red one," Edward pointed down the street. "Can you walk that far?"

They were kind, both of them, too kind. They made her feel like a hot, cross baby wrapped in too many warm shawls. She wanted to kick out, to be free. She was not a baby any longer. She had traveled between two worlds. She had out-faced Prosson and saved the life of the infant he would have dashed to the ground. She had waved goodbye to a boy she might have loved, had she been older and more fond of cabbages and cows. She had crossed the dreaded Time Wreck and survived. All she had not done was to bring back any proof of this, except two stale sandwiches and a thin book nobody would be able to read.

She couldn't bear it! She couldn't bear going back to being Spooky Loonie, whom nobody believed. She pulled away and ran off into the night. She could hear their worried voices calling after her, and footsteps following, but she knew this part of Islington better than they did, and once around the corner, ducked immediately behind the pillars of a dark doorway and watched them go past.

"Mary! Mary, where are you? Come back!"

She ran all the way to Cloudsley Towers, with Calabal padding beside her. She heard the church clock strike ten and tried to remember everything that had happened on that night, which seemed to her so long ago. She'd been writing in her diary. Then she'd had a bath. Mum and Dad were at the cinema. They wouldn't be back till after eleven. They wouldn't even have missed her yet.

"I worried about them, Calabal, when I was in your world. I thought of them every night. I thought of Mum crying and Dad standing looking out of the window, waiting for me," she told the dog. "They would've been frantic. I was away so long. What has happened to that time? Where's it gone?"

Swallowed by a timequake, as if it had never been. And here she was, dressed in the clothes Dafre had given her, with her bare feet, soundless on the pavement, taking her home. Nobody had missed her. No anxious faces looked out of the windows, hoping to see her. She had come back too soon. It was quiet on the top floor of Cloudsley Towers. Faint lights shone through the glass panels in the three front doors, but that did not mean anybody was in. They always left the hall light on at night, whether they were there or not.

Her key was on a chain round her neck. She pulled it out and opened the door. Calabal pushed past her and stood for a moment sniffing the air. There was a smell of lemon bath salts —

I had a bath before Mum and Dad came back from the cinema.

There was someone in the bathroom now. She could hear a small, tuneless voice singing, "Alone, all alone, With no love of my own. . . ."

Calabal's ears pricked up. He looked up at Mary and then back at the bathroom door, as if puzzled, and whined softly.

The singing stopped. There was the sound of splashing as somebody got out of the bath. A voice called, "Mum? Dad? Is that you?"

Mum and Dad came back earlier than I expected that night.

What would happen when they came? Would they see her? Would they see Calabal? Or would they only see the girl in the bathroom, the girl who had taken her place?

Am I a ghost? Did that last quake wipe me out?

The bathroom door opened and a girl stood looking out at her, another Mary with curly red hair and frightened black eyes, a squeaky-clean Mary, wrapped in a pink bath towel, who said in a terrified whisper, "Go away!"

29

Mary couldn't be frightened of herself. For that was all the other Mary was, herself as she'd been the day before she'd gone away. What a scared little mouse she'd been then. Listen!

"Keep that horrid dog away from me!" the girl cried, trying to shut the door on Calabal, who wanted to push past her into the bathroom.

"He won't hurt you. I expect he's thirsty. He'd better not drink the bathwater though, not with that stuff in it. Come along, Calabal, I'll give you some fresh water in the kitchen."

To her surprise, the other Mary followed her and stood watching from outside the kitchen door while she filled a soup bowl with water and put it down for Calabal.

"Mum won't like that," she remarked. "Her best bowl."

"She's got five others like it."

"How do you know?"

Mary turned to look at her. "Who do you think I am?" she asked.

The other Mary looked frightened again. Her hands clung onto the doorframe as if for life. "I dunno," she said. "You can't be my ghost. I'm not dead. Besides, that don't look like a shroud you're wearing exactly. Though you're covered with dust like you come from a tomb, so maybe it is. Go away! I don't want to die."

"Nor do I, though it looks like one of us has got to go. Unless —"

"What are you?" the other girl cried. *"Why have you come here to frighten me?"*

"I didn't," Mary said. "I just came home. As for who I am, haven't you guessed? I have. I'm you and you're me. Me as I was several weeks ago. I've been to the other world where our great-great-grandma went, and come back. Only I've come back a day too soon. That's why there're two of us. I and I. Mary past and Mary future. Don't go to Coram's Fields. I've already done that."

The other Mary was staring at her indignantly. "But I want to find Mary Coram's world. I want to prove —"

"You have. I have. We're the same person. *No! Don't let go of the door frame. Don't come any nearer!*"

"I can't help it. I feel something pulling me toward you."

"I can feel it too. That's why I've wedged myself behind the stove. We mustn't touch each other."

"Why not? What would happen?"

"I dunno. I think we might sort of merge and become one. Like the drops of mercury. Remember Mr. Rogers showed us in the lab?"

"Yeah." Mary Past was silent for a moment, then she said honestly, "I don't understand. It's a bit confusing, isn't it? If we become one person, will we be me, not having gone anywhere, or you, having just come back? And anyway, won't we be bound to go to Coram's Fields again, because that's what happened? Then we'll vanish and come back and vanish and come back forever."

"No, we won't," Mary said stoutly. "Because when we merge, you'll know that it was pretty frightening at times over there. I can tell you, I'm glad to be back safely. Don't be afraid you've missed out. When we merge, you'll know everything. Bound to. You are me. It's just, you see, I haven't anything that will prove for certain that what I say is true. Remember what it's like to have nobody believing you? Gally said it shouldn't matter if you know it's true yourself, but I dunno. . . . Why should everyone else be wrong and me right?"

"There's me too."

"You don't count. You are me. We've got to convince somebody else. Just one other person would do. You see, I couldn't carry much in my backpack, not without their guessing I was going to run off. So I've only got an old book in a foreign language nobody will be able to understand, and my autograph book and two stale sandwiches I didn't have time to eat. I don't think that's going to do the trick, do you?"

"So you want us to remain apart until somebody sees the two of us, and then they'll know we're telling the truth?"

"Yes," Mary said, smiling, pleased to find she hadn't been completely stupid eight weeks ago, or however long it was. In fact, she thought, looking at her past self, I wasn't so bad at all. I'm quite a nice-looking girl, when I'm clean.

"They'll have to believe us then, won't they?" she asked. "Let's go — careful not to touch me. Now you go first! Let's go into the sitting room and wait for Mum and Dad to come."

Freda Timpson knew Mary lived in Cloudsley Towers, but she did not know the number of her flat, and they could find nobody to ask.

"Let's ring this doorbell," Edward suggested. "Perhaps they can tell us."

But the old woman who opened her front door on a chain and peered through the chink with a suspicious eye did not know the Frewins. "Never heard of them. A young girl with curly red hair? Dunno. My eyes are not so good. What's she done?"

"Nothing. We were worried about her. Is there a doorman who could tell us the address?" Freda asked, but the woman had shut the door firmly, and they could hear her footsteps shuffling away.

"Shall I ring again?"

"No. Let's try someone else."

But there was no answer from the next two apartments they tried, and at the third one, a child's voice called out, "Go away. I'm not allowed to open the door to anyone. Not even if you say you're a policeman. Not even if you're the queen."

"Do you know the number of Mary Frewin's apartment? You can shout it through the door."

"No, I can't."

"Why not?"

"I don't know it."

They laughed, and bidding the child goodnight, walked out of the block again, looking for another entrance where there might be a doorman. But it was Mr. and Mrs. Frewin they found, standing waiting for the elevators on the far side of the block. Freda recognized them at once, from open house at school. The very large, limping man and the tiny birdlike woman at his side were easy to remember, even though the woman's hair was now dark, not blonde.

She ran up to them and then hesitated, not knowing what to say. Perhaps they were the sort of parents who didn't care what their children got into when they were out. Perhaps Mary was allowed to roam the streets at night, dirty and unkempt and wild. Then she remembered the look in Mary's eyes, dazed and shocked and bewildered.

"We wanted to have a word with you about Mary," she said.

"Now?"

"If we may. We saw her about ten minutes ago, but she ran off. I don't know whether she's home yet —"

"Mary? Can't have been Mary you saw. She's been home since tea time," Mr. Frewin said. "Got her friend Isobel to keep her company and Mrs. Frayne only next door to keep an ear open for them till we come back. She's a good girl. She wouldn't go out on the sly, not Mary."

The elevator came down then, and on the way up to the top floor, Freda told the Frewins how she and Edward had met the girl and spoken to her. Of course she knew Mary, the child was in her class. She knew her well. And Edward had met her too and spoken to her about her ghosts —

Mrs. Frewin, who had kept shaking her head in disbelief, suddenly looked worried. When the elevator stopped, she raced out and along the passage, dropping her bag in her anxiety to find her key. It was Mr. Frewin who opened the door with his key. Immediately they heard a dog barking and a girl's voice hushing it.

"Mary?"

"Here, Mum!"

The voice came from the sitting room.

The two parents reached it first, with the two teachers following more slowly on their heels. Even then, they could all have seen the two Marys, had it not been for Calabal. The dog, straining at his collar and barking, distracted Mrs. Frewin's eyes. She screamed. Mr. Frewin pushed her behind him, nearly knocking over the teachers in the process. By the time the three of them had sorted themselves out and the dog had been quieted, it was too late. All they saw was the dirty girl in the odd clothes standing smiling at them, her face bright with love. At her feet was a crumpled pink bath towel.

"Dad! Mum!" she cried, rushing over. "Did you see? Did you? Do say you did!"

"See what, dear?" her mother asked, and the two teachers looked puzzled.

"Oh, *Mum*!" Mary was close to tears.

Then Mr. Frewin, who trusted his eyesight, said slowly, "I saw two of you — two Marys — and I haven't been drinking. One sitting in that chair over there, wrapped in the pink bath towel that's now on the floor. And one in that chair opposite, in those peculiar clothes you've still got on. When we came in, they both got to their feet and stepped toward us. Then, well, it happened so quick. Difficult to describe. They came together like they was drawn, like a pin to a magnet, clunk! And then there was one. Call me mad if you like. I can't explain it, but that's what I saw."

"Oh, Dad!" Mary cried, hugging him. "You're not mad. It happened like that. It did! Oh, I've got so much to tell you! Oh, I'm so happy to be back."

Not everyone who heard her story believed it. Her father and mother did, of course. They made a fuss of Calabal because he had saved her life, and they arranged for one of Dad's friends to look after him until they could find an apartment with a garden. Nonny believed her and wished he'd been with her. Isobel said she was struggling with her doubts.

The Bad-Dog Boys still called her Spooky Loonie, but she no longer cared.

Edward Potts was fascinated by her adventure. He recorded it on tape. He asked her endless questions, most of which she could not answer.

"Mary, why didn't you ask?" he kept saying plaintively. "Oh, I wish I'd been there!"

"Well, you wasn't," she said, her grammar slipping, as it often did when she was cross or excited. "I did ask questions. I found out a lot of things. . . ."

She had learned how to milk a goat and make cheese. She had learned two-and-a-half lines of poetry and nearly fallen in love. She had learned that a wicked man like Prosson could be speckled with odd kindnesses, as if bits of his childhood were shining through the grime of years. But this wasn't the sort of thing he meant.

"I learned a lot about time," she said sulkily. "Only it's too complicated to explain to somebody who hasn't been there."

"I think you've done splendidly," Miss Timpson said warmly. "I shall never quite trust my watch again." And she frowned at Mr. Potts, who quickly apologized, saying he'd been carried away. He then asked Mary's permission to make a photo-copy of the book Belois had given her, so that he

257

could show it to Professor Bancroft, who was an expert in deciphering unknown languages.

She nearly said no, he couldn't. But he looked at her so hopefully that she didn't have the heart to refuse.

"He didn't mean to make me feel stupid, but he did," she said to her father later. She often confided in her father now. Dad never got in a fuss. You could tell him things.

Her father laughed and said he knew how it was.

"When I was a young man in the army, I could be stationed in a foreign country for weeks and hardly learn the names of its cities nor two words of its language nor its principal exports. I was too busy keeping alive. People forget you've got more important things to find out first, like who you can trust and whether the road is mined or the water fit to drink. Oh, you learn things all right, you learn a great many things, some good and some you'd sooner not know." He looked at her. "I expect it was like that with you, Mary. You had other things to worry about. I hate to think of you all alone, and frightened."

"It wasn't bad, not once I'd made friends." She thought of the sunlit garden, the warm milk, and the sweet bread — and Gally smiling at her. "It wasn't bad," she said again.

"It sounds bad enough to me. That madman Prosson —! You took a terrible risk trusting him, Mary, after everyone had warned you against him."

"Somehow I had a feeling he wouldn't hurt me. You see, he kept confusing me with Mary Coram. Calling me by her name. I told you how they said he'd created a legend out of her story and had fallen in love with her, even though they'd never met, even though she was dead. Sounds silly, I know, but Mum says that sort of love must be the hardest to cure — no varicose veins or burnt toast or forgotten birthdays, just a star shining bright forever."

"Your mum said that?" Mr. Frewin said, surprised. "I hope that doesn't mean —" He was silent for a moment, looking a bit depressed.

"She said it wouldn't do for her. Too cold. She said she preferred a real man, even if he burnt the toast every morning."

"Did she really say that?"

"Yes. Dad, about Prosson, I had to ask him to show me the way back. I had to take the risk, didn't I? What else could I have done? I wanted to come home."

He put his good arm around her and held her

tight. "When I think what might have happened! When I think we might never have seen you again!" His voice sounded choked. Looking up at him, she was surprised to see the glint of tears in his eyes. "We're so proud of you, Mary," he said. "Mum and me, we're so proud of you. How you managed to keep your head on that wreck, I don't know. How you thought of those strips of paper — I couldn't have done it."

Pleased and embarrassed, Mary said, with an airy wave of her hand, "Oh, it was nothing." Then she laughed, seeing her father's expression, and confessed, "I was scared silly, Dad. I've never been so scared before in my life."

"It's sensible to be frightened of something dangerous," he said, as he had always done when she was frightened.

"I remember the first time you said that," she told him. "I was a little kid, yelling because there was a greenfly crawling up my bib."

"Dangerous things, greenflies. Ask any rose," Mr. Frewin said, smiling.

Early one morning, Mary went down to the canal by herself, to the place where she most often used to see her ghosts, as she'd called them. They seemed fainter now: soon she'd be too old to see them anymore. Her friends had gone. Gally and Belois, Dafre and Keet and Kollos. There was nothing left but shadowy fragments: a hand here, a knee there, a pair of small brown feet limping — limping!

"Jippy!" she shouted, waving and laughing. "Jippy, it's you, isn't it? See, I got home safe."

For a moment she saw him quite clearly, the small Neptal boy with a huge, happy smile on his face, waving back at her.

"Take care of yourself!" she shouted.

He nodded his head and vanished. She stood for a moment, remembering them all, wondering if she'd ever see them again. Then she turned and walked home through the autumn sunlight.

Author's Note

The Red-Eared Ghosts is truly more of a time fantasy than it is science fiction. To write it, I read books on physics by Stephen Hawkins, Ervin Lazlo, and John Gribbin. But when I found the physicists didn't agree with each other, I gave up and began inventing an alternate world, time-quakes and all.

Five centuries ago, a fault developed in the space-time and electromagnetic fields near London, causing, as it were, a new skin to grow over the damaged tissue. This formed a second, much smaller world, which though roughly parallel in time, developed independently. Its inhabitants, originally people from our world who'd blundered into it before the barriers between the two worlds had hardened, continued to live in a simple agrarian society. In the 1800s the Neptals arrived from a distant and more advanced planet. Their spaceship crash-landed into the fault at its weakest part near the barrier between the two worlds and played havoc with the space-time and electromagnetic fields, causing timequakes and earthquakes and a series of great fires that destroyed Izel and most of the population. Into this confused and damaged world, Mary Frewin's great-great-grandmother, Mary Coram (Crumb), arrived by chance. Mary had a force of character that the Neptals admired. When she died, she was not forgotten, but remained a source of both inspiration and superstition.

The wreck of the crashed spaceship was at the epicenter of the timequakes. Here space-time is chaotic: past, future, and present are so muddled that the traveler through the wreck can step into his own death or pass his babyhood into an unborn state with no warning. Only the dog, with his superior instinct and sense of smell, was able to avoid these pitfalls. But Mary Frewin would have arrived home at the right chronological time had not a timequake overtaken her at the last moment, destroying the weeks she'd been away and bringing her back to Islington the day before she left it.

So although physicists might not agree on the principles put forth in this novel, I hope readers can enjoy my flight of imagination and can envision this very different but parallel world.

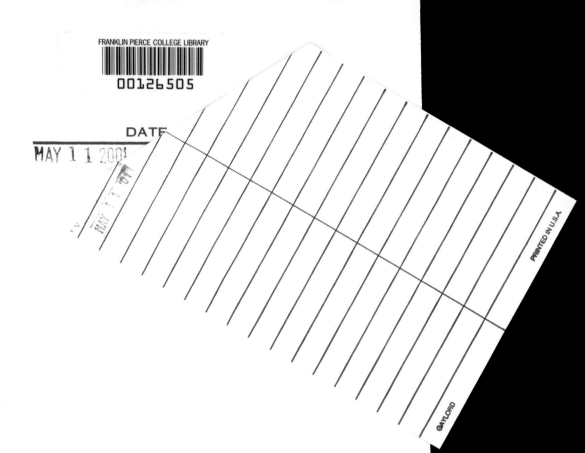

PRINTED IN U.S.A.

GAYLORD